TEUTONIC TALES

TEUTONIC TALES

by

BONNIE BARRIGAR

Everlasting Publishing
Yakima, Washington
USA

Teutonic Tales
by
Bonnie Barrigar

ISBN-13: 978-0-9983858-6-0

Second Edition
Everlasting Publishing
P.O. Box 1061
Yakima, WA 98907

TABLE OF CONTENTS

RHINESONG 1

SWAN OF THE RHINE 85

THE SWANLING 133

REDEEMED 156

TWO BROTHERS 167

BETTE 171

SUMMER GREEN 174

THE MAN ON THE WHITE HORSE 176

VETERAN'S DAY EVE 179

RHINESONG

Chapter One

The year was 1984 and the world lay in the frigid depths of The Cold War. No where was this ideological split more evident than in Germany which had been cleaved, with the Red Army sickle, into a capitalist West and a communist East. Even this nation's former great capital city of Berlin lay sundered, wounded, and schizoid.

No one in either Germany felt the pain of this wound more keenly than West Germany's newly elected Chancellor, Alaric Schwan, as he rode in his private zeppelin to as close to East German air space as he dared fly. It was a cool, but bright day in early November, and the entire landscape sequence of concrete city buildings, wooden farm houses, and barbed wire-sheaved guard towers which rolled out beneath him was bathed in the amber glow of autumn sunlight. But amber often signals caution. Not surprisingly, every mile of land leading up to the infamous Berlin Wall seemed to flash the yellow light of warning.

To be sure, Chancellor Schwan felt caution as his bespectacled blue eyes took in the length of the relentless, steel-reinforced barrier which was uncoiling like a gray serpent under his airborne vantage point. He also felt strong loathing as he continued to gaze down on The Wall which had divided farmers from their land and brothers from each other. Involuntarily, Herr Schwan's small chubby fingers

1

clutched the globe-shaped goblet of cognac he was holding as though he meant to crush it and his small, handsome face took on a look of bitterness. He had brought a bottle of the elegant brandy along with him on his cross-country zeppelin flight to share with his CDU Party Officials in celebration of his election victory the day before. Now he felt like anything but celebrating.

Just then, Herr Schwan's black mood was relieved somewhat by the presence of his friend and CDU Party Vice-President, Horst Flugel, who had stepped up to join him at the central front window of the airship's passenger car. Only four inches taller than the Chancellor himself at 5"6', Herr Flugel, with his plump, rounded physique, short wiener fingers, greasy complexion, and frank disposition, seemed like a living combination of the multitudinous varieties of sausage for which his native Stuttgart is famous. Even his thick, medium-brown hair seemed to have the texture and hue of lockwurst. Flugel had been Schwan's closest companion and associate ever since their pre-political days when Schwan had been West Germany's wealthiest and most prominent rock music promoter and Flugel had been his highly capable talent scout.

"Why do you look so glum, Alaric? I should think you'd be as happy as pie now that you're Chancellor," remarked Flugel to his chief in his blunt, comradely way.

"Horst, I can never be truly happy as long as this remains standing," Schwan told him grimly as he continued to stare down with resentment at the ugly, concrete barrier between East and West.

But the diminutive Chancellor was in a much better mood later on when he was back again behind his heavy oaken desk at his Bonn Chancellery office. He was his usual take charge self, puffing on small French cigars as he issued orders and discussed government matters with that same zeal, persuasiveness, and amicable authority which had enabled him to win contracts and influence clients during his years as President of his Karussell Platte AG record company. Now at age forty-five, he had a country to run.

"Herr Chancellor, I suggest that we mend the economy by having more money printed," ventured Schwan's raw-boned, goateed Economics Minister, Gunther Stieglitz.

"No, Gunther, that would just make the present inflation worse. The only cure is a wage and price freeze," said Schwan as he left the white velvet swivel chair behind his desk and began to pace the off-white plush rug which he had just had the Chancellery's main office furnished with. As he paced, the little fellow puffed away on his cigar in a most determined manner.

"Big industry isn't going to like it," warned Herr Stieglitz who was standing some distance from his small statured chief and directly under one of the Audubon swan paintings which Schwan had hung on his office's oak paneled walls.

"People sometimes don't like what's good for them, Gunther. So if you're really serious about ending our country's economic woes, do your best to assist me in pushing a wage and price freeze bill through the Bundestag(Parliament)," said the blond Chancellor who had stopped in midpace to fix his Economics Minister with one of his most persuasive smiles. With his right hand, he forcefully and as though for emphasis, snuffed out his imported cigar in the white swan-shaped ashtray which graced his desk. This gesture was not lost on Herr Steiglitz who could see that underneath his boyish charm and smooth manner, Schwan had the toughness of an iron eagle.

"I'll do my best to see that such a bill is passed, Herr Chancellar," promised the Economics Minister who then proceeded to join Schwan in drawing one up.

For the rest of the day, Schwan conferred with each one of his ministers in this way and in the process had several unusual, but effective measures set in motion. To combat wide spread air pollution, which was daily shriveling up West Germany's historic forests, he proposed a nationwide gasoline tax and the implementation of a more expansive public transit system as an alternative to cars. For increasing and seemingly insoluble nationwide unemployment Herr Schwan also had a solution – build-up the country's defense industry and educate people of all ages to work in it in some capacity.

"But the Russians will pop their corks!" exclaimed Flugel when he heard his chief spell out the above policy.

"So, let them pop," said Schwan with a defiant toss of his pale-blond, early Beatles-style haircut.

Of course, to deal with the Russians, who wanted to maintain a monopoly on military power in Europe at that time, the little Chancellor insisted that more US missiles, nuclear and otherwise, had to be based on West German soil. That is, until his nation's soon-to-built armament factories could produce their own.

"Alaric, think of the flak we'd get from the Green Party over this issue," protested Flugel. "Remember that open air rally at Kiel where they threw whole cartons of rotten

4

eggs at the last Chancellor and that was just for having a new nuclear power plant built there. These environmentalist fanatics are death on anything nuclear and they've got clout. They could even turn the youth of West Germany against us."

"Horst, when will you ever stop doubting? Our credentials with the youth segment will always be second to none because of our pasts as rock music impresarios. And as for those Green Party idiots, they don't frighten me. I know enough about their leaders' secret drug dealings to put them all behind bars. And if they give us any trouble, that's where they'll go," laughed Schwan as he leaned back on the edge of his desk and puffed away on his cigar in a manner that was at once casual and masterful.

Astute as he was, Schwan was aware that some of his more radical and austere proposals were unlikely to be popular at first with the West German public. But he and Flugel were old masters in the art of forming and manipulating public tastes and ideals, and so the newly-elected Bundeskanzler felt justifiably confident that his people would continue to support him through thick and thin.

His lifelong personal friendship with United States President, Hank Robins, also weighed heavily in his favor, at least as far as world affairs were concerned. Tall, handsome, urbane, and possessing the keenest memory that Schwan had ever seen in a human being, Mr. Robins represented the best of America to the diminutive Chancellor. Furthermore, the two men shared many things in common. Besides being very, very conservative in outlook, both of them happened to be scions of their countries' entertainment industries – Robins as a former actor and Schwan as an erstwhile rock star.

But great as Schwan's admiration was for the United States and its Chief Executive, his deepest, most heart-felt loyalties naturally lay with Western Europe. One of his grand schemes was the eventual creation of a United States of Europe – a continental merging based on NATO and the European Common Market with West Germany, France, and Italy presiding as the joint leading nations. Not surprisingly, this was the topic which Schwan immediately brought up when his ministers broached the subject of foreign policy. It wasn't surprising either that the little Chancellor had discussed his plans for creating a U.S.E with every European leader who had phoned him to congratulate him on the day of his election victory. All of them seemed pleased with the idea and promised to meet with him to discuss it further as soon as they could arrange it. All of them, that is, except British Prime Minister Barbara Thrush who feared that such a political, military, and economic merger would bring about the loss of British currency status.

"She's a real tough customer, that Thrush, and she's probably going to buck you every inch of the way on that European Unification issue," remarked Flugel to his chief shortly after the "Iron Lady" had politely, but firmly declined his offer.

"Oh, she'll come around, Horst. I'll just have to be patient and find the right approach to use with her," said Schwan who knew that he could sell practically anyone on practically anything once he had found their most vulnerable spots.

Now three days later as his third day at the Chancellery Office was drawing to a close, Schwan topped things off with a conference concerning his pet project of European Unification, along with a discussion of which CDU (Christian Democratic Union) Party officials should or should not comprise his new cabinet.

Then when all was said and done for the day, the small German leader left the large, gray, squarish Chancellery Building and all of its personnel and boarded the white Mercedes Benz which would take him to his lavish estate house in the suburbs of Bonn.

As his down-white car, which bore a silver swan ensign on both of its front doors and on its hood, sped off into the frosty faded golden light of November's alpine glow, Schwan could not have known it but his movements were being watched with the eyes of baleful hatred. Or rather, a single hate-filled eye, for the tall, lanky young man in the black leather trench coat who was staring so balefully after Schwan's vehicle as it disappeared down the gullet of the city like a white sugar lump, had only one icy-blue eye. His other eye, which happened to be his left eye, was obscured behind a large black leather eye patch. So large was this patch that it covered most of the left side of his unsalubriously pale thin face.

"Someday soon I'm going to kill you, you little devil. And I know exactly when and how I'll do it," muttered the somewhat spectral young man, his breath in the cold early evening air trailing out like vapors of ectoplasm.

This phantom, who was wearing a black leather visor cap over his blond Ziggy Stardust haircut and black leather boots and riding breeches beneath his trench coat, was none other than Winsoln Auslaugen – a former rock opera composer who loathed Schwan to the verge of madness. His quarrel with the little fellow began in the glittery decadent Seventies when platform shoes and "glam rock" were the vogue and Schwan was still only the mogul of his Karussell Platte music company.

A native of Munster, Auslaugen had joined the West German Army, through much circumvention, at the age of seventeen. Eighteen was supposed to be the minimum age for Bundeswahr recruits. Being quick of mind, tough of body, and a hard worker, Auslaugen soon proved himself to be an excellent soldier with a special knack for handling explosives. So his superiors assigned him to the Demolitions Corps where he quickly worked his way up to the rank of Sergeant Major. Ten years later, Auslaugen was on his way to being promoted Brigadier General, but it was then that his restless spirit tired of army life and he decided to leave it for a musical career. His time was long up and he was free to step back into civilian life any time he desired.

This career shift was not really that out of character since Auslaugen had always shown a remarkable gift for writing music, especially of the rock-classical variety. As a schoolboy, his teachers often caught him scribbling the notes of rudimentary, but quite good songs and musicals on lesson paper when he should have been paying attention to the black board. At their insistence, and with his family's encouragement, he began taking an adult level course in piano song composing at the age of eleven. Later on as a youth, Auslaugen had tried to lay aside his musical interests and devote himself exclusively to a military vocation. But the Spirit of Music already possessed him and would not be exorcised. He found himself jotting down musical scores during his off-duty hours and he couldn't resist spending his leave time taking in musical events.

Then at age twenty-seven, he decided to let his profound talent and compulsion for music take the lead in his life's destiny – to go "whole hog" so to speak. So shortly after leaving the service, Auslaugen took the money he had accumulated over the years from his military paychecks and rented a studio apartment in Bonn where he set about writing his first full-length rock opera.

This masterpiece, when it was completed, surpassed Wagner in drama, Debussy in ethereal sweetness, and The Moody Blues in the tasteful merging of old music with new music. Auslaugen gave it the title of Faustine and its plot centered on a cunning Fifteenth Century French courtesan who sold her soul, along with those of her many lovers, to the Devil for wealth and eternal beauty. Having five acts in all, the opera had taken the composer two years of hard work at the piano to complete.

Having a premonition that his rock opera was sure to set the West German music world on fire, Auslaugen lost no time in bringing it to the attention of Schwan who was the West German equivalent of Phil Specter at the time. Being the shrewd appraisers of music that they were, the little Entrepreneur and Flugel had listened to the audition tapes of Faustine which Auslaugen had sent them and liked what they heard. So it wasn't long afterward that Schwan contacted the tunesmith from Munster and invited him to come and sign a contract with him at his Karussell Platte AG office which stood in Bonn's residential section and on the side opposite to where Auslaugen's inner city apartment lay.

"Your brilliant classical-rock opera has H-I-T written all over it," Schwan had told Auslaugen quite heatedly over the phone.

That same day, Auslaugen had met Schwan at the blond tycoon's elegant main office with its medieval blue, white, and silver tapestries of swans and heavy gothic furniture. For hours they discussed *Faustine* and Auslaugen's plans for it while Flugel looked on, endlessly smoking American-made cigarettes and now and then offering a suggestion or two. Finally, a deal was worked out to the satisfaction of both parties – Schwan would publish, record, stage, and promote Auslaugen's opera, while Auslaugen would reap a huge royalty percentage – and the two men signed a contract.

Herr Schwan had tried to be fair with Auslaugen in all of his dealings with him, but the young composer was naive and egocentric which made a dangerous combination. Being rather inexperienced as far as the business side of the music industry was concerned, Auslaugen had been willing to let Schwan take the lead in both the promotion and production of Faustine. He had even agreed to this in the contract they signed together.

But as time progressed and the songs from Faustine started to become hits, Auslaugen became jealous and possessive of his creation. Suddenly, he wanted the whole thing done his way and that's when Schwan's problems with him began. When the little Entrepreneur had one of the songs from Faustine, "Is It Love Or Money", sung by a tenor instead of a bass, Auslaugen had let him know of his extreme displeasure in a volley of letters and phone calls. When Schwan had the blonde ballerina in Act Two replaced by a raven-haired gypsy dancer, the temperamental tunesmith had thrown a tantrum of Jim Morrison-like proportions.

"How dare you cast some black-haired bimbo in the role of Giselle, The Dancer!" he exclaimed in a furious phone call to the diminutive music promoter.

"Now look here, Winsoln," said Schwan who talked in a firm, but soothing voice, hoping that he could make Auslaugen calm and see reason. "A gypsy girl dancer is the most appropriate character for the scene, era, and place in Act Two. And besides, remember the terms of our contract."

"To the Devil with you and that contract!" Auslaugen all but shrieked as he brought the telephone receiver down with an ear-bruising crunch.

For a time, Schwan gave in to Auslaugen's demands concerning Faustine, but he soon found that doing so was commercially impractical. So he took charge again of all affairs connected with the musical production, but this, of course, only made the composer more irascible and contentious. Auslaugen began to make threatening phone calls to Schwan's office and even sent him letters saying that his days were numbered. The little Entrepreneur countered this by warning Auslaugen that he would sue him for both breach of contract and harassment if he didn't cease and desist hassling him.

These warnings quieted Auslaugen, but it was with the quiet that comes before a mortal storm. For months, the tunesmith from Munster sat in his studio apartment doing little but brood bitterly over the way that he had, he felt, been ruthlessly swindled in his dealings with Schwan. Being in the ugly mood that he was, he certainly didn't feel like writing any more music, but instead could be seen staring for hours with calm malice at the royalty checks which Schwan still kept on magnanimously sending him. And as he continued to do this, his hatred for the diminutive fellow grew and flourished in his heart and mind like some dark poisonous mushroom.

It counted for nothing with Auslaugen that the royalties Schwan was having mailed to him, plus his savings from his army days, all added up to a fortune. To a man of his tem-

11

perament, the only things that truly mattered were absolute control of his creations and purity of art, as he interpreted it.

Then a year later, in the spring of 1975, while he happened to be lounging in his black leather armchair sipping heavily sugared coffee and reading the evening news in his gray smoking jacket, Auslaugen received a most horrible inspiration – a fool hardy, horrible inspiration.

This "inspiration" came in the form of an ad in the "Employees Wanted" section of Bonn's most prominent newspaper, Der Zeit. It read this way,

Singers And Musicians Wanted

> We at Karussell Platte AG are now hiring male singers and musicians for our new production of Kismet. Men of dark appearance with the ability to speak Arabic need only apply. Come in person to our Condor Studios for auditions any work day between 8:00 am and 6:00 pm. Phone 444-8537.

The moment Auslaugen's icy blue eyes lit on the above ad, he knew he could even the score with Schwan.

Chapter Two

The next day, the temperamental tunesmith went to a local costume shop where he purchased a collar-length black wig, a pair of polaroids, and some make-up. Then with these purchases in hand, he had returned to his apartment where he put on a pair of bell bottom jeans and an oriental-style blouse. Then he began working on his face and hands. Standing in front of a full-length mirror, with a frame made of Norwegian wood, he placed the black wig over his Ziggy Stardust haircut, and dark tan colored make-up over his pale complected face and hands. His pale colored eyes he hid under the dark sunglasses. On his feet were leather loafers instead of sandals since it was still early spring and therefore rather cool outdoors. Luckily, he had picked up a few Arabic words from a Palestinian exchange student he had gone to high school with. When Auslaugen was through putting on his disguise, the whole effect was really quite convincing, especially since he had a bit of a hooked nose.

"My, and don't you look to be the right proper Saracen," remarked Auslaugen to himself as he looked his altered form up and down with pride.

Then he had put on a denim jacket along with a pair of rubber galoshes and picked up his guitar, plus a few other items which musicians don't usually take to auditions, and he was off to Karussell Platte AG's Condor Studios in his black Volkswagen bug.

As he drove the ten miles between his downtown apartment and Schwan's recording studios, the composer suddenly and for seemingly no reason at all began to remember a World War I era poem which he had once read in an old edition of the British humor magazine, *PUNCH*. This poem was titled, "Hades Telephone Conversation", and went like this,

> "The Devil was snoozing, softly snoring,
> When he heard the phone;
> Kaiser Bill was on the other end talking,
> Wondering if he was home;
> Said Kaiser Bill, 'It's time you helped us',
> At The Somme the British nearly scalped us;
> Asked The Devil, 'Will you sell your soul?'
> 'Yes!', said Kaiser Bill,
> 'If that will help my wartime goal!'
> So The Kaiser sold his soul,
> But it did him little good;
> In June his troops still met defeat,
> At the Battle of Bellau Wood."

Then with a wry smile he pushed the satirical poem out of his mind and forced himself to concentrate on his plot against Schwan.

After he had arrived at the imposing white granite gothic structure which housed Schwan's empire of printing presses, record presses, offices, guard's quarters, and movie and music studios, he parked his car and left it to join the huge line-up as it slowly shortened, being drawn in through the door like a sparrow sucking in a caterpillar. While he stood on the sidewalk, the young composer had endured a light sprinkle of spring rain and the friendly approaches of his line-mates, most of whom were real Arabs and who thought that he was one of them. They made comments to him in their own lyrical oriental tongue, which Auslaugen understood but sketchily, and offered him cigarettes, which he never smoked. Because he wanted to be alone with his own thoughts, Auslaugen considered the attentions of these men a nuisance. However, he replied to their comments in polite, though monosyllabic Arabic and refused their smokes in a kind manner. So before long they just let him be to mull over what he was conspiring.

Finally, the line had dwindled down, and it was Auslaugen's turn to go through the door to Condor Studios. But instead of turning left and heading for the audition room where Schwan stood waiting loftily on a gilted balcony with a pair of earphones on his small, proud head, Auslaugen turned right and made a bee line, quickly and stealthily, for the business' central office which he knew would not be very well guarded at the time. From past experience, he knew that during auditioning most of Schwan's company guards, Der Schwagwahr, would be removed from other areas in the business complex and stationed near the Entrepreneur in the audition room. The composer had been wise to come in disguise. Not only did he blend in with the crowd around him, but Schwan had ordered his Schwagwahr to bar his presence from his Karussell Platte AG et al., ever since their falling out over Faustine.

To begin with, the luck of The Devil seemed to be on Auslaugen's side. He had made it into the main office without attracting curiosity. Once there, he had overpowered Klara Seetaucher, Schwan's pretty, buxom, brunette Secretary, with a handkerchief full of ether. Then he had rifled through the filing cabinet which contained every contract Schwan had ever signed until he found the one he wanted – the hateful document he had signed with the little tycoon in which he promised, in writing, to give Schwan complete control of his opera. This, he quickly stuffed into his billowy blue and gray shirt as he hurried for the nearest exit with his

15

guitar still in hand. The contract he planned to destroy the moment he reached his flat.

But just then, Auslaugen's luck began to change for the worst.

"Hey, rag head, the auditions are that way!" called out one of Schwan's gray clad guards who had just spotted Auslaugen and thought he was a singer coming for the auditions who had lost his way. As the tall, husky man spoke he gestured in the direction of the audition room.

Knowing that the gig was up, Auslaugen broke into a long-legged run, but this served to excite the guard's suspicions. His galosh shod feet had hardly hit the pavement outside the business building when the muscular man grabbed him by the collar. Acting with swift reflexes born of military training, Auslaugen pulled out his army pistol and leveled it at the guard threateningly.

"Unhand me, kalb (dog)!" he screamed with a noticeably fake Arabic accent.

But the Schwagwahr, who had also been well-drilled, instantly knocked the gun out of Auslaugen's hand. As this happened, the distraught composer lost his black wig, the contract, and some of his brown make-up. The sentry then recognized him and an all-out fist fight ensued between the two men. Not long afterwards, several more Schwagwahr joined the sidewalk brawl and Auslaugen, despite his military training, was soon too battered and bruised to put up any further resistance.

The guards then brought the much black-eyed and disheveled Auslaugen before a furious Schwan and a tearful

16

Ms. Seetaucher who had only just regained consciousness. The little Entrepreneur wasted no time in having Auslaugen arrested by the regular police.

Auslaugen was then immediately apprehended on charges of breaking and entering, assault, robbery, and yes, harassment and breach of contract for Schwan now had no qualms about finally pressing these long overdue charges against him. In due course, the composer was tried and sentenced to twenty- five years in Rabenkeep, Bonn's high security prison.

When he was assigned his cell on Block 39 of Rabenkeep, Auslaugen was both profoundly bitter and disillusioned. He was also, predictably, furious.
Furious that Schwan had thwarted his plot to destroy their contract and even more furious that his small adversary had placed him in prison. However, his belief that the little tycoon could not keep on winning against him forever kept him from giving into discouragement, as did his cellmate, Otto Steintopf. Herr Steintopf, an ornithologist turned to crime, was a stout, homely little man of about fifty with a balding head of black hair and the longest nose Auslaugen had ever seen. But despite his considerably comic appearance – he looked as though his father had been a fat oompa band player and his mother a penguin – the fellow was a master criminal with a sardonic sense of humor.

For years, the "birdy" little man had been the terror of Bonn and thereabouts, ingeniously using birds of all kinds as accomplices in his bank robberies and smuggling schemes. He had been apprehended many times before, but always seemed to think up a clever new way of escaping. Yes, Herr Steintopf was a regular Houdini when it came to jail breaking.

After Auslaugen's anger at the world, and Schwan in particular, had cooled down somewhat and he began to feel more sociable, he really began to like Staintopf. He quickly warmed to him, as much because of his dark sense of humor as because of his genius as one of their nation's top crime lords. This last time, it had taken the police years to locate and arrest him after he had slipped all of the gold out of a local refinery, and then only with the help of his worst foe, Detective Bruin Fledermaus. True to his sardonic humored temperament, Herr Steintopf had once sent Det. Fledermaus a wooden plaque on which a stuffed bird lay, like a prop out of the horror flick Psycho, with both of its feet curled up. By the bird lay a metal plate which read, "Now I've given you the bird!" Steintopf on his part was drawn to Auslaugen's raw-boned toughness and pronounced ingenuity.

As time and their sentences drew on, the two men grew increasingly more fond of each other. It enhanced the closeness they enjoyed as cell mates that they always ate their meals together in the Rabenkeep cafeteria, exercised together (although Herr Steintopf naturally hated to exercise), and helped each other in the laundry room where both of them had been assigned.

When their prison duties were done for the day, Auslaugen and Steintopf went quietly back to their mutual cell where the younger man would sit for hours on his cot listening with fascination as his birdman friend told him of the criminal capers he had pulled. It was at such a time, when the lights were low and the block guard was snoozing, that Herr Steintopf whisperingly informed Auslaugen that he was about to pull off another prison break.

"May I accompany you? As you know, Otto, I have a score to settle with someone on the outside," Auslaugen asked eagerly under his breath.

"Yes, you may, Winsi. But it'll be very risky," warned Steintopf in an undertone with a devilish twinkle in his round gray-blue eyes.

"Risky? I was in the army, remember? And to us soldiers risk is our bread and butter!" said Auslaugen excitedly without managing to raise his voice a notch.

"Good, my friend. You are just the bird I need to help me in my escape plan," whispered Herr Steintopf as he laid his pudgy hand with avuncular affection on Auslaugen's shoulder.

The next morning, the tall man and the short man went to work at the laundry as usual, but this time they had something other than scrubbing clothes in mind. While Auslaugen distracted the guards and the other prison inmates with a clever, but funny song about a lovesick cuckoo bird, Herr Steintopf snuck over to where the naptha, which was used for dry cleaning, was stored. In seconds there was a terrific explosion and the whole laundry room was choked with a curtain of acrid, blinding smoke. Under this cover, Auslaugen and Steintopf both made a quick and successful escape – Auslaugen to return to his apartment and Steintopf to return to his underworld henchmen and plan another caper. Auslaugen couldn't resist wishing him luck.

The convict-composer snuck into his apartment under the cover of darkness to find to his relief that his landlord had not yet rented it out nor had even had his possessions carted out. Moving quickly, he shed his prison uniform for a tunic, riding breeches, and boots, all of black leather. His black wig completed the disguise along with the polaroids. Upon leaving, he took with him a leather satchel full of explosives and related equipment.

Under a mask of darkness, he made his way on foot and in the most roundabout way back to Schwan's business complex which he knew wouldn't be heavily guarded at the time, it being Sunday evening. Like a true friend, Herr Steintopf had arranged their prison break so that Auslaugen wouldn't have to wait to pull his own caper.

Locating the all but deserted music publishing building, Auslaugen forced his way in with a crowbar and began to set up a line of explosives. His intent was to cripple Schwan's business, while exacting a heavy personal revenge on him by destroying the printing presses which had published Faustine to the tycoon's satisfaction. Schwan's record factory would be next.

But just as he was in the process of laying out his first and smallest explosive device on a dormant printing press, something totally unexpected happened. Before he could have so much as detected her presence, Schwagwahr Führerin Christina Tag, Schwan's blonde, petite, but dynamic and fanatically loyal Schwagwahr Commander and younger sister, had stalked up behind him and kicked him head first into his explosive. The impact caused the device to go off, but it was Auslaugen's head which received the force of the explosion, not the printing press which he had been about to destroy. Auslaugen shrieked, lay for a moment, and then staggered upright, the left side of his face a mass of shredded flesh and what remained of his left eye looking like a collapsed red star. Blood was running down the front of his leather tunic in crimson rivulets. Small though she was, Fraulein Tag was a woman of very tough fiber. Even so, seeing Auslaugen standing before her all torn and bloody made her involuntarily cringe away from him and be stricken momentarily speechless.

Empowered with the energy which can only be born of extreme pain, Auslaugen took advantage of Tag's temporarily imbalanced condition. He knocked her out of the way and then was far away from the vicinity of Karussell Platte AG before she had a chance to come to and send for her gray uniformed personnel.

Blinded by his pain and still bleeding, the injured composer continued running. But he wasn't just running blindly. He knew that the river Luxemburg lay a mile away from Schwan's business complex and as soon as he found it, he threw himself into it seeking cooling relief and cleansing for his horrible wounds. He swam languidly in it and before long it had swept him into the bricked, nitrous interior of Bonn's storm sewer. Though he felt more dead than alive, he slowly pulled himself up out of the water and lay in the driest part of the sewer's dark interior.

Chapter three

For two days, the stricken composer lay there shuddering, moaning, and healing. But tough, healthy, and quick-healing though he was, he knew that he would need medical attention or else die of a possible infection. With this urgency in mind, Auslaugen resolutely combed down his shaggy blond hair so that it adequately covered the raw left side of his face and then painfully and slowly, but determinedly made his way on foot to the nearby town of Beuel where Dr. Dieter Krane lived. Dr. Krane, who had befriended Auslaugen during his army days, had once been a military doctor. Then too, he also loathed Schwan, though for less personal reasons.

"Why Winsoln! You've been seriously injured! What – who could have done this to you?" said Dr. Krane who was genuinely shocked by the extent of Auslaugen's wounds. Not only had flesh and muscle been torn, but bone had also been shattered.

"Schwan did this to me!" ground out Auslaugen through his pain and exhaustion.

"Then that little blond iniquity will have to pay!" vowed the doctor as he gently, but skillfully began the cleaning and disinfecting of the whole left side of his friend's face and head. In his heart, he feared that Auslaugen might have suffered injury to his brain so deep did the splintering of his skull go. But he would not voice this fear to his patient. At least not yet.
In reply to Dr. Krane's earnest vow about making Schwan

pay, Auslaugen looked up drowsily into the studious face of his benefactor. In his dazed eyes, the visage hovering over him seemed almost angelic with its firm jaw, gray mustache and pompadour-style hair, and concerned deep brown eyes. He smiled up at Dr. Krane before fainting dead away.

But having the constitution of a sea gull, Auslaugen was far from dying, despite the gravity of the injuries he had sustained at the Karussell Platte AG publishing house.

For several months, Dr. Krane, who was an excellent general practitioner and plastic surgeon, carefully and skillfully nursed Auslaugen back to health. He repaired the tunesmith's shattered facial and head bones. He stitched together his torn and blasted muscles and flesh. But Auslaugen stopped short of letting him perform plastic surgery on him.

"No, Dieter, let me keep these scars so that the whole world will be able to see what sort of demon Herr Schwan is," insisted Auslaugen to his doctor friend.

Of course, Dr. Krane could have done nothing to restore his busted eye. So he did the next best thing for him. He had a special eye patch made out of black leather which was large enough to cover not only his damaged eye, but his enormous mass of scars as well.

Along with extensive surgery, Dr. Krane helped heal his musical friend by providing him with good food, much rest, and fond companionship. Then when Auslaugen was almost completely on the mend, Dr. Krane began to provide him with something new – a dose of political indoctrination.

For Dr. Krane was a communist. Auslaugen, although he had never taken a direct interest in politics, was nevertheless, of a very patriotic bent and therefore deeply distrusted communists and what they stood for. He had not known of his friend and benefactor's conversion to the extreme left wing ideology and so hearing Dr. Krane speak in support of it came as an enormous shock to him. At first, Auslaugen turned a deaf ear whenever his companion quoted from Karl Marx's "communist bible", Das Kapital, or launched into a lecture about why he believed the Soviet Union and East Germany had the better way of life. But because he was in an exceedingly weakened position and condition, both physically and spiritually, he eventually succumbed.

Before long, Auslaugen himself was reading Das Kapital and integrating its philosophy into his own belief system. He even began to attend meetings with Dr. Krane of the Bonn Chapter of the West German Communist Party. It was then that he started seeing Entrepreneur Schwan as someone even more hateful. Not only because he had, he believed, been personally wronged by him, but now also because being a wealthy, powerful businessman, he exemplified all that was hateful in the capitalist system. As Auslaugen now saw it, not only did Schwan need overthrowing, but the whole economic system he represented needed overthrowing. Dr. Krane saw this new attitude in Auslaugen and encouraged it.

The tunesmith now turned radical evidently had suffered some brain damage in the explosion that had ripped half his face away. This manifested itself in severe headaches and occasional fits of temporary madness which were to bedevil him for the rest of his life. His face would always wear a pinched look of pain. But these symptoms were neither debilitating nor life threatening, so the young former composer was soon going to places on his own in Dr. Krane's gray and blue Porsche.

Most of these included colleges and tea houses where Auslaugen had been tipped off by his fellow "reds", for he was by then a card carrying communist himself, that he would find people who hated Schwan and who were ripe for radicalization. Using his newly blooming leadership qualities and powers of persuasion, he sought these people out and soon had a growing multitude of followers. To them, he was known solely as the Trugbildführer. This was the name he would be going by publicly from then on. Winsoln Auslaugen had been declared legally dead after the episode at Schwan's printing establishment and so the erstwhile tunesmith had been content to let that name die as he had supposedly done. His choice of the "Trugbild" feature of his new name was as fitting as it was eldritch. Trugbild is the German word for phantom.

Of course, Auslaugen gave the name of Trugbilder to his following. He even had special costumes designed for himself and them which Dr. Krane was happy to supply them. These costumes, "uniforms", as Auslaugen called them, were somber in appearance to say the least. Thin black leather pants disappeared into thigh high zippered black leather boots, while the sleeves of their black leather high-collared tunics disappeared into long black leather gloves. Sometimes they wore a black leather visored cap. At other times they donned a black enameled helmet with a black visor which covered the entire front part of their faces and ended in front in a curved point like a bird's beak.

"I wish Otto could see me now. I look very like a bird myself in this uniform," remarked Auslaugen with amusement to Dr. Krane as he saw himself in the mirror for the first time wearing his Trugbildführer uniform. Little wonder then that when Auslaugen had a flag made for his paramilitary group it depicted a black, sickle-bearing vulture on a solid red background.

Several times a week, he and his Trugbilder would meet at the widespread country property of a "party friend" where he would put them through a series of grueling military drills. Then afterward, he would lead them all to the basement where he would give them a lecture on Marxist-Leninist doctrine and revolution.

Outwardly, the group existed for the purpose of opposing Arch-Capitalist Schwan, but secretly their purpose was for the destruction of the whole capitalist system in West Germany. Dr. Krane and his other fellow communists understood Auslaugen and supported him wholeheartedly, even to the point of supplying him and his group with weapons, ammunition, and military training equipment.

But it wasn't only his own countrymen who recognized Auslaugen's extraordinary potential. Dr. Krane also brought him to the attention of an operative from Moscow who met the Trugbildführer secretly at the doctor's swiss chalet-style home and was both intrigued and impressed by him.

"What would you give to overthrow our capitalist foes?" Konstantin Kurlov, the beetle-browed, burly Soviet agent inquired testingly.

"Anything that was required of me!" replied Auslaugen with a fanatic's earnestness.

"Anything? It is your hard work and loyalty that we want, comrade Trugbildführer," said Kurlov as he fixed the German with a stare full of fire and ice.

"You may have that along with the hard work and loyalty of my Trugbilder," promised Auslaugen who knew that he had a powerful friend in Kurlov.

"Wonderful! You are a smart young man, comrade, and if you stand by us you will really go places," said the Russian with a broad predatory grin. He wasn't kidding.

Moments later, Kurlov produced a document from the pocket of his trim, burgundy, double breasted suit. The document pledged loyalty to the Kremlin in return for the Kremlin's full support. The tall, stocky Soviet invited Auslaugen to sign it and he did without the slightest hesitation, thereby selling his soul so to speak.

It is ironic to note how closely Auslaugen's political climb had been paralleling that of his nemesis all during this time. For during the time that the composer had joined the Communist Party, Schwan was becoming affiliated with the CDU Party. When Auslaugen became Trugbildführer, Schwan was starting on the campaign trail leading to the office of Chancellor. It was as if Auslaugen was some dark, sinister political alter ego of the former record tycoon. Of course, the volatile young man from Munster had forsaken music for the nonce.

Now on the third day of his being Chancellor, Schwan thought not at all of Auslaugen as his chauffeured, small, but elegant car rolled unto the pebbled driveway of his private estate which he had named Schwanengarten. He was thinking of his family and pets, both of which he had a king sized amount of.

This estate, which covered a whole city block by itself, was crowned by a towering Gothic mansion with twenty rooms, many pointed arches, delicate stonework, and several stained glass picture windows. These colorful, exquisite windows all depicted scenes from the opera, Lohengrin, in which swans predominate as motif. The whole mansion was made of down-white marble, as was the ten foot wall which surrounded it. Beside the mansion was a barracks, all made of oak wood, in which Schwagwahr Führerin Tag and her paramilitary army had their headquarters. But this barracks was no faceless, austere building. Called Der Schwagwahr-keep, its wooden exterior was heavily polished and carved all over with intricate scroll work and the same general ornate designs as the mansion itself bore.

While inside, the Schwagwahrkeep's oak paneled canteen and sleeping quarters had the look of similar rooms in a financially well off boy's boarding school. There were even authentic heraldic plaques on every wall and here and there a standing suit of armor. Sometimes, there were even crossed swords on the wall which had once belonged to a Medieval knight, lord, or even king. Of course, many of these heraldic plaques, suits of armor, and swords had actually been part of the Schwan Family legacy since the days of old when knights were bold and barons held their sway.

Then upstairs, like the quarters of the headmaster, presided Christina Tag's private quarters. These were comprised of a heavy, though ornately carved oak desk, walls lined with books, most of them concerning military tactics and German history and mythology, and a large, four square, oaken bed. On this bed was a satin spread in the tricolors of the West German flag with the Federal Republic's black eagle embroidered on it. While above the bed and on four squarish oaken pillars was a satin canopy done in the same red, yellow, and black bands of color. On Tag's desk was an antique revolving globe from the 12th Century, yellowed with

28

age and in every niche of her bookcase stood a weapon of some sort.

As anyone who attempted to be a threat soon discovered, thirty-five-year-old Tag could be very tough and even ruthless in her defense of her brother and his property. Even so, there was another side to her as well, for she was very pretty and liked to add subtle feminine touches to her military dress and décor. She always wore her blonde hair long and with a slight curl and was fond of jewelry with rose-shaped settings. Roses were one of the motif themes she surrounded herself with. Indeed, a bouquet of roses always graced her oaken desk.

"They remind me of that folk song, 'Roeslein Auf Der Heiden'. I grew up listening to that tune and though it was written long ago, for me it will never grow old," she would explain during coffee klatches with her family and friends.

Indeed, the young lady took much interest in all things cultured. She was exceedingly fond of Wagnerian opera and whenever she went any place in her field gray, chauffeured Audi, she would listen to Wagnerian arias on the car's cassette player as she rode.

Schwan had returned his sister's intense loyalty with genuine fraternal love and had looked after all of her needs ever since the death of her movie star husband, Richard Tag. By her late husband, Ms. Tag had two sets of beautiful blond twins whose names were Erik, Erika, Adolf, and Adolfa. Of course, they stayed in the white marble mansion where a servant cared for them. When she had time, she gave all of her love to her children, but her duties prevented her from being with them as often as she and they would have liked.

Directly outside of the Schwagwahrkeep, which Tag shared with her personnel, stood training facilities for the Schwagwahr and a good-sized munitions dump. In front of the Schwagwahrkeep was an authentic 17th Century cannon with a neat pile of five cannonballs from the same era beside it.

After Schwan had arrived at the arched oaken door of his mansion and rapped once with the large, gold-plated, lion's head door knocker, the door swung open to reveal the beautiful, peaches and cream face of his wife,

American-born April. Beside her were the joyous faces of two of their six children, Herman and Heinrich. These two charming little boys of three and five had taken after their auburn-haired, hazel-eyed mother in coloring. Beside them was towheaded eight-year-old Erika, whom Alice treated no differently than the other two. Neither Tag nor Alice, nor any of their children were the least bit jealous of each other. In fact, Tag would have been there as part of the family welcoming party had she not been obligated to be present that night to oversee the installation of a new cadre of Schwagwahr guards at the Chancellery.

Within seconds Schwan's four other children, together with Tag's, had joined Herman, Heinrich, Erika, and their respective mother and aunt. After they had sufficiently welcomed Schwan, all of them went together to the enormous family dining hall. In the center of this long room stood a lengthy oaken table draped with a silk, swan-patterned table cloth of the frothiest white. On this table was the finest silver cutlery, while above it shone four, three-tiered crystal chandeliers like star tiaras. Masterfully painted swan murals completed the lovely picture.

The widespread meal which greeted the large family was a deliciously typical German supper of konigsburger klops, sauerkraut, fresh apples, tea, and chocolate cake. Following their meal, during which Schwan and the others had talked long and warmly about what each one had been doing that day, all of them played a game of monopoly together. When their game was finished, they paid a visit to Schwan's upstairs aviary – which included among other wonders – a penguin and a cockatoo. Then they retired to their beds, the younger children bedding down first with a tucking in and a bedtime story from the little blond Chancellor.

But though it was Alice's lovely white arms that Schwan fell to sleep in the comfort of that night, his thoughts were not only on her but also on the members of his own Schwan Clan and his own bizarre past.

The Schwan family of Bavaria, whose heraldic emblem was, of course, a swan, was an illustrious, wealthy, armorial one whose scions could trace their ancestry back to the Ninth Century. The great-grandfather whom Schwan had been named after, Alaric The Bold, had even been made a Baron by King Charlemagne. In the Eleventh Century, a branch of the Schwan family had settled in Cluj, Romania, which was how Entrepreneur Schwan came to be related to Romania's stellar Opera Diva – Leda Lenescu. Tall, slender, Leda Lenescu whose cascade of black hair, dark charms, five-octave voice, and versatile singing style inspired him to pull many complex political strings so that she could leave the iron grasp of her now communist homeland long enough to record on his Karussell Platte AG record label.

All in all, the Schwan Clan was one with great roots in both history and music. Ironically, at the turn of the century, it was music which brought one of its finest sons to a tragic end. Professor Leopold Schwan, who happened to be the little tycoon's grandfather, was a composer of truly prodigious talent. In fact, it was from this grandfather that the Entrepreneur seemed to have inherited his own musical gifts along with his small, blond, boyish good looks. This composer of twelve breathtakingly beautiful operas between 1889 and 1912, he lived a happy and successful life and was an accomplished and well-recognized artist in his own time. That is until he met Gustav Geier, the crooked, greedy, ruthless head of Geier Publishing House.

Not knowing Herr Geier's true character, Prof. Schwan had entrusted his lifework, the seven act opera, *Christina's Heart,* to the balding, stoop-shouldered buzzard of a man who then promptly stole it. When the enraged Professor of Music threatened him to his face that he would press legal charges against him, Geier responded to his threat by attempting to silence him forever with a drenching of nitric acid. That was the last straw for poor Prof. Schwan.

Maddened by pain, the loss of *Christina's Heart*, and the cruel injustice of his situation, the composer managed to find his way to the main sewer system of Bavaria. There in its cold stygian tunnels and recesses, he had died of his injuries and of a broken spirit only a few months thereafter.

Leopold Schwan's horrific fate had deeply affected his son, Helmut, and his other children, Anna and Hartmut. All of them had been under twelve years old when the tragedy happened and were so deeply affected by it that they, later on as adults, went to Munich where they attended Bavaria's finest medical university. Their shared mission was to become doctors so that they could help treat burn victims of all kinds. Then they moved back to their ancestral village of Partenkirchen where they established a joint, family-run medical clinic.

Entrepreneur Schwan, son of Helmut Schwan, had been deeply affected also by the horror which had happened to his grandfather, although this could only have been on some subconscious, genetic level, since the unfortunate Professor had been dead long before the little fellow was even conceived. On one level or another, he definitely had been greatly influenced by what had happened to his musical predecessor. Seemingly from birth, he was obsessed by fears of being burned, of disfigurement, and of dank, dark, underground places. He certainly hadn't caught these fears from his father, uncle, or aunt for they had spoken very little of this subject around the small, plump, fair boy during his toddlerhood.

Nor had he been born in the clinic which his father and uncle and aunt had established together. His mother, Klara, had been an opera singer which was why, perhaps, he had been born on the evening of April 20, 1935 in Partenkirchen's Goldenvogel Opera House in between performances of Wagner's, Die Walkure, in which the stellar Diva, Lotte Lehman, was the singing heroine. Furthermore, he had been born in the lyrical-voiced lady's own dressing room, along with his twin brother, Atwulf. His father had delivered him and Atwulf, but had needed to use Miss Lehman's silver, stork-shaped embroidery shears to cut their umbilical cords, since he had lost his surgical scalpel down the furnace grate of the opera house just prior to their birthing.

Nevertheless, their delivery, in which the lovely opera star herself aided Dr. Schwan as an unofficial maternity nurse, went quickly, safely, and easily for both themselves and their mother. They emerged bawling as two of the roundest, pinkest, and healthiest boy babies once could imagine. Although they were full- term, both of them were considerably under-sized. Their father was not the least bit concerned about this, however. Being small was a trait that ran in his family.

The Schwan family was traditionally Roman Catholic, as are most Southern German households. Therefore, Alaric and Atwulf's parents took them to their village's handsomely built St. Michael's Cathedral frequently. In fact, it must have been there, amidst the stimulation of the cathedral's three-tier pipe organ, the white and black robbed priest's solemn liturgical chants, and the choir's ethereal voices, that the two little boys first felt an awakening of their inborn musical talent. Before they could even talk, the infant twins tried to sing along with that heavenly-voiced choir.

All in all, despite the phantom shadows of their grandfather's gruesome end and the fact that the Second World War came all too soon with its food rationings, air raid drills, and other major traumas, the little blond twins enjoyed a happy and secure early childhood. What made their young lives truly happy was the fact that their father had been, at the age of forty, too old to be called into the Wehrmacht and, therefore, was able to be with them whenever his doctoring duties didn't call him to the Schwan Family Clinic.

Alaric and Atwulf spent their early childhood days playing with their big sheep dog, Hansel on the cobblestone walk or on the well-tended grass of the lawn beside of their family's big oak mansion. Often they played tag and similar games with other children and when they were a bit older, they were each given a bicycle. One of their favorite pursuits was to play roll-a-hoop together on the sidewalk.

The twin boys had other more serious pursuits as well. When both of them were four years old, their father hired a tutor to give them at-home preschool training. He also hired a music teacher for them, for he and his wife could already see that their young sons possessed prodigious budding musical talent and they wanted to do everything they could to encourage them. There was no sweeter sight nor sound than Alaric and his brother, with their little, round, blond heads together, singing Engelbert Humperdinck's holiday lullaby, "Christmas Town", in a duet.

> "Full of joy with ne're a frown,
> I will live in Christmas Town;
> Christmas Angels gather near me,
> When I pray, they always hear me;
> Christmas Town, Christmas Town,
> I will live in Christmas Town;
> Like Christmas stars my eyes do shine,
> And in my hair is snow so fine;
> On my brow a holly crown,
> I will live in Christmas Town;
> Christmas Town, Christmas Town,
> I will live in Christmas Town."

Not surprisingly, their singing this piece before friends and relatives, and even as a part of a school outdoor caroling team, became a yearly Schwan family Christmas tradition.

On the evening of December 24, 1940, this winter holiday took on an even deeper meaning when Alaric and Atwulf's little sister was born. For them and their parents, the beautiful, lively, blonde girl child was the sweetest Christmas present Divine Providence ever gave them. So they all agreed that she should be called "Christina". Naturally, the birth of this daughter brought a new sense of completeness and happiness to the whole Schwan family.

Chapter four

In 1941, the bliss of this family was shattered again, this time by way of a more further reaching violence. Alaric Schwan would never forget that horrible night when the British war birds made their flight of destruction over Partenkirchen. When the town's chief Air Raid Warden gave notice to everyone that the first of these bombers had been sighted, the entire Schwan family had made a frantic beeline for the cellar. But none of them had been fast enough.

As the haunting phantom wail of the air raid siren wafted through the starless black air, the whistling of the falling bombs could be heard all about, and then came a terrific rumble which shook the sturdily built oaken Schwan family mansion like the pounding of Thor's hammer. An instant later, it had collapsed like a child-built structure made of wooden tinker toys. Alaric blacked out.

When he came to, he found that he was bruised all over but that, luckily, not one bone of his was broken. He was, however, laying in a hospital he had never seen before. Beside him, fluffing out his pillow, was a nurse with short silvery hair whom he had never seen before either. But she had kindly gray eyes and so set his newly conscious mind at ease.

As soon as she noticed that Alaric was awake, this nurse, whose name was Frau Annelise Pfau, brought him a bowl of warm delicious chicken vegetable soup along with some little white soda crackers in the shape of chickens.

Because the boy was too bruised in the arms to want to lift his spoon, the good nurse fed him the soup herself. While she did so she explained, in as gentle a voice as possible, that he had been hurt in the air raid of the night before.

"But, don't worry, young fella. Your injuries aren't bad and you will back playing street tag soon," Nurse Pfau assured him with a tender smile. "Your sister Christina too has survived, but her injuries were so slight that after the doctor thoroughly looked her over, he sent her from this hospital to a special girl's home in Berchtesgaden right away. God has blessed both of you."

The whole town of Partenkirchen, Nurse Pfau went on to explain, had been leveled. Even St. Michael's Cathedral had been left a pile of shapeless rubble. No medical facilities had been left standing, including the clinic run by Alaric's own family. Which was why he was now laying in a hospital bed in the nearby town of Oberammergau.

When Frau Pfau told Alaric that his beloved St. Michael's Cathedral was now no more, tears began to stand out in his bright blue eyes. Then when she told him that he and his little sister were the only survivors of the raid on his family's mansion, his tears began to pour like the rain when it bursts just before the hurricanes which sometimes assault the coast near Hamburg. Continuing in a soothing tone, his nurse explained to him how after the British bombs had stopped falling, the chief Air Raid Warden and his crew had set to work clearing away the debris of the shattered Schwan Mansion. Underneath the mass of wood, glass, and plaster they found the broken bodies of Alaric's parents, his Uncle Hartmut, his Aunt by marriage, Frieda, and his four cousins, Dietra, Maxina, Christopher, and Lotte. Alaric, they of course found alive but unconscious with the hysterically bawling Christina in his arms. So they had these two remaining children taken to the Taubchen Hospital in Oberammergau, along with twenty other survivors of the Partenkirchen air raid. His Aunt Anna and his twin brother, Atwulf, had seemed to have just disappeared.

"But don't worry, dear, even though you are an orphan, The State will see that you are given a good place to live, just like your sister has," Frau Pfau told the boy with a gentle smile as she spooned him the last drop of soup.

For a week or two, six-year-old Alaric stayed in Taubchen, quickly recovering from his head to toe bruises under Nurse Pfau's kindly conscientious care. At the end of that time period, one of the Taubchen doctors pronounced him physically healed of the effects of the horrible night raid. Although mentally and emotionally his cure had not been so thorough. Perhaps it never would be.

On the day of Alaric's release, Nurse Pfau had brought him a brand new field gray uniform for him to wear. Once he had donned it, she happily informed him of where his next destination was to be.

"Be proud, dear boy, for you are going to Adlerfelsen," she said the word "Adlerfelson" with the kind of exultant pride which a Medieval queen sometimes expressed as she sent a young knight off on some grand adventure.

Because he had grown to like Nurse Pfau and because she had been so happy and enthusiastic about this place called Adlerfelsen, Alaric figured that it had to be a capital place indeed and so looked forward eagerly to going there. He was even whistling and walking with a spring in his step as he said good bye to her and boarded the gray bus which was to take him and ten other boys the forty-five miles from Oberammergau to Adlerfelsen in Munich. As he rode, he stuck-up cheery conversations with the other youngsters all of whom were of assorted ages and sizes, but every one of whom had on the same sort of field gray shirt, matching knee pants and long socks, and brown leather lace-up boots that he was wearing. They too seemed to be happy and excited about where they were being taken that day.

However, Alaric was soon to lose the enthusiasm he had shared with his bus mates. Although Adlerfelsen was an orphan home for boys established by the wealthiest and most influential people in Southern Germany's Nazi Hierarchy, it did not look that way to him. The whole building complex was a spartan, squarish, utilitarian structure both inside and out with gray curtains at the windows and that color dominating everything.

Alaric Schwan, who was used to finer surroundings, didn't like the looks of it. He was to feel even more uncomfortable once he actually started living at the barrack-like Adlerfelsen. He found the firm cots which he and the other boys were given to sleep on awful, along with the steady diet of bread and vegetables which was the sole fare served at the Munich "boy's home". In all fairness to Adlerfelsen's patrons and proprietors, it must be pointed out that the above cheerless diet was the result of wartime blockades and rationing and not due to intentional cruelty or neglect on their part.

Even worse than the menu for Alaric were the cold showers that he and his fellow Adlerfelsen inmates were forced to take at all times of the year. To "toughen them up", they were told. The long marches in all kinds of weather were a pain too, especially in the feet. Then too, although they were certainly humane – they let him visit Christina every holiday and often gave him a pat on the back or some words of encouragement whenever he did a job well – the field gray uniformed caretakers at Adlerfelsen were stern, no-nonsense types by nature. Of course, discipline was strict.

But little Alaric was a real trooper at heart and before a year was out had adjusted very well to the austere environment of Adlerfelsen. Possessing high intelligence, he eagerly took in the thorough education which the institution's schoolmaster, Erwin Falkner, offered. He even tolerated being spoon-fed Nazi propaganda, while secretly keeping his own belief system. The more he was forced to at least put on the mask of submission to his Führer, the stronger grew his faith in his mother church and Christ Jesus. Under his breath he would say his rosary and voice his confessions and penitence. This hidden devotion kept him strong mentally, emotionally, and physically as well as spiritually.

What also contributed to the towheaded boy's bodily health was that he genuinely enjoyed playing soccer and mock military games with his fellow students in the wide Adlerfelsen playground. Luckily, all of the other boys were so fond of his companionship that not one of them thought of putting him down because of his baby face and lack of statue.

Alaric also coped with the regimental harshness of his surroundings by turning again to music – an activity which his humorless caretakers seemed surprisingly happy to encourage him in. They helped him further develop his singing, piano playing, and music writing abilities. In the process, his musical skills became so good that he eventually brought lighthearted cheer to the hearts of the most dour staff members of Adlerfelsen. He also began to learn how to develop a charming and persuasive personality.

Because of these new traits of his, the boy was soon treated with special favor by the orphan home's proprietors. They brought him out to show off his musical talents whenever a visitor came to Adlerfelsen. These guests were always surprised and delighted to see so much talent in one so very young.

Once, after a piano rendition of Wagner's "The Ride of the Valkyrie", which he played in honor of and for the enjoyment of Herman Goering, the mountainous Air Marshal had been so moved that he hugged the boy and then gave him a toy fighter plane. When he happened to be touring Munich, Der Führer himself would occasionally drop by to be regaled by a concert by Adlerfelsen's towheaded musical child genius, and whenever he did, he always brought chocolate candies which Alaric adored.

Alaric's caretakers also began to do favors for him, small and large. Finding out the he could influence and manipulate people this way, through both his personality and his music, gave him growing self-confidence. He was already developing the management skills which would be very valuable to him later on in life.

As his tenth birthday neared, Alaric looked forward to joining The Hitler Youth Group. Every day, he had been dreaming in happy anticipation of donning a brown uniform, beating on a drum on which colorful flames had been painted all around, learning to use a rifle, and taking part in all of the other activities which belonging to this politico-military organization would entail. Yes, with his perfect love of music, Alaric especially looked forward to using that drum. How proud Christina would be of him!

But while entertaining these fancies, the boy remained true to his belief in God. While he would take on the trappings of a nazi, to him it would all be just another show. An outlet for his music. He might just as well be playing a drum in a carnival or as part of a side show. Then too, the Soviet Red Army was on a march which was drawing closer to his homeland and he was willing, young as he was, to take up arms against them since he viewed them as "Godless invaders". This was not contrary to his religious upbringing. Then too, had he been ordered to use his gun against civilian Jews, or civilians of any sort, he would have cleverly found a way to dodge that order. He was a young boy with a mind of his own.

However, fate was going to step in and Alaric was not going to be forced to make such decisions either way. For it was around the time of his tenth birthday that his country was defeated by the Allied Forces and forced to surrender unconditionally. Furthermore, the British, French, American, and Russian Military Administrators, who now held the authority over occupied Germany, quickly put all Nazi Organizations, The Hitler Youth included, completely out of commission. This certainly was a disappointment to the young Alaric, but no wheres near did it match in intensity the heartache which the defeat of his beloved fatherland brought him; especially when he saw it being carved up between the victors like some enormous Easter goose.

Predictably, Adlerfelsen changed hands – the former caretakers being replaced by American ones and its name being changed to Eisenhower Waisenhaus (Orphanage). Although their manner was more tolerant, laid-back, and full of a sense of humor than his erstwhile caretakers, Alaric had at first resented the new, foreign staff of his orphan home. But when he found that playing them Glen Miller tunes and other "stateside" Hit Parade Songs made these Yankees go as doty and indulgent over him as the Nazi staff had, he began to warm to them and before long he liked them as much as they liked him. Beside, he was deeply, truly grateful that they weren't Russians who had always epitomized to him all that was brutal, barbaric, and uncouth.

"Hanns, I can't complain about the Americans who now run this place. They treat us well, which is more than those nasty commies would do. I shudder to think what must be going on in the eastern part of our country now," confessed Alaric to one of his boy's home companions after the latter had told him how much he disliked having "damned Yankees" over him.

Shortly after his twelfth birthday, Alaric was taken out of Eisenhower Waisenhaus by a distant relative named Emil Klausse, who had also taken charge of the by now seven-year-old Christina. Of sturdy build and possessing the white, collar-length hair, bushy white mustache, and yen for cigars of a Teutonic Mark Twain, sixty-year-old Herr Klausse was a distant cousin of the children's mother. He was also a wax sculptor of much talent and ingenuity and the figures in his Zurich "House of Wax Personalities" rivaled the best of Madame Tussaud's. He waited out the Second World War in Switzerland, but as soon as it was over he had returned to Bavaria with plans to move all two hundred of his life-like masterpieces into a new wax museum he was already having established in Munich. Herr Klausse had also come seeking Alaric and Christina, whom he had been trying to track down ever since his return to his homeland.

A bachelor who had never had children of his own, Herr Klausse provided Alaric and his little sister with the best food, clothing, and paternal love that he could. He even tried

43

to give them companionship. The three of them frequently went out on hiking and fishing jaunts, although it was some-what hard for an out of shape man of his age to keep up with a healthy twelve-year-old boy and a seven-year-old tomboy.

And what a lively little girl Christina was turning out to be! Already, she was showing the interest in police work that was to remain with her for the rest of her life. She loved reading detective stories, playing cops and robbers, and watching police shows on TV. For her eighth birthday, the adoring Herr Klausse bought her a police woman's costume, equipped with a shiny badge and a toy pistol that came with its own holster and shot caps. Christina was so proud of it that she would put it on right after coming home from school and then, with the visored Polizei Cap over her halo of blonde curls and carrying her little uniformed and booted self with an air of conscientious authority, she would patrol her yard – sometimes on foot and sometimes in the wooden go-cart-style Polizei car her brother made for her.

"Halt, everyone, and don't move!" she would suddenly sur-prise Herr Klausse and Alaric by blurting out. "A crime has been committed!"

Christina, her brother, and their elderly benefactor now lived together in a gingerbread-style house in the heart of Munich and just across the street from the old fellow's soon-to-be wax figure gallery. When it was finally completed and furnished, the wax people in it never ceased to amaze and stimulate the interest of the boy and girl.

From the beginning, Alaric's and Christina's new mentor saw that their every need was fulfilled. Education for both of them was given top priority. Christina began studying at a grade school which had been established especially for bright girls, while Alaric was enrolled at the best second- ary school in Munich. The boy was twelve by this time and starting to need glasses, possibly because of over study, and so Klausse had him promptly supplied with a pair. The elderly wax sculptor stopped short of legally adopting his young charges, however. This was because he knew that Alaric and Christina had an inheritance coming to them from their father, that is, what little of it happened to be left after the war, and he didn't want to spoil their chances of receiv- ing it. So the old gentleman became their fatherly guardian instead.

As such, he made sure that more than the children's mundane needs were taken of. Herr Klausse was a devote Catholic himself and went with the boy and girl to the local church every Sunday and said Mass beside them. He made sure that they observed every holiday with Christ and His Holy Mother in mind.

Because of his caring nature, Alaric and Christina had loved the paternal old fellow from the moment they met him. The little girl had been drawn to his solid kindliness and the love and security he radiated. For her, he was, as though rolled into one, the father and uncle she had loved and lost at such a young age. While Alaric was fond of the man's artistic spirit, empathetic manner, and even his aromatic cigars which he never seemed to be without. From the ven- erable wax crafter, the boy not only learned to appreciate the art himself but even learned how to assist his guardian in the fashioning of the deceptively lifelike figures. In the process, Alaric discovered that he had quite a flair for wax sculpturing himself.

But music was the art form in which he continued to shine and the one in which Herr Klausse wisely encouraged him the most. One of the ways the gentleman did this was by buying him a grand piano shortly after he had taken up residence with him.

"Stay with your music, my boy genius, and the world will hear from you someday," promised Herr Klausse with a puff on his ever-present cigar and an affectionate twinkle in his faded blue eyes as Alaric thanked him for his most thoughtful and apropos gift by playing him his favorite piece of music, Bach's "Toccata and Fugue in D Minor", right then and there.

Another way Herr Klausse encouraged the boy was to ask their Priest if he could play their church's massive, booming, pipe organ for every service. Father Johann agreed to let the boy play a series of complex hymns in a private recital and was so pleased with his performance that he slated him to play every Sunday and holiday from then on.

The old man's prediction was to be fulfilled sooner than either he or twelve- year-old Alaric could have anticipated. Only two years later, when he was fourteen, the boy tunesmith was "discovered" by a talent scout from a prominent Bonn-based record company who had heard him performing an original song called "Swan of the Rhine" in a high school talent show. The talent scout's name was Marti Von Fildmann and the record company which he represented was no less than Karussell Platte AG.

At Herr Von Fildmann's promptings, Herr Klausse and Alaric joined him for a trip to Karussell Platte's company headquarters to meet Heinrich Schmidt, the recording business' shrewd, all-powerful head, for the purpose of a possible recording contract for the teenaged musician. Alaric's little sister, who had no musical talent nor desire to develop any, stayed behind in Munich with a family who were personal friends of Herr Klausse.

"Why do you want to sing, my boy?" was the first thing that Herr Schmidt said to Alaric after he had been introduced to him.

Frail, hawkish, but nevertheless, almost imperious in manner, the eighty-six-year old tycoon placed great stock in how serious and committed his clients were to their music. He was therefore determined to test the boy and so discover his level of commitment to his art.

"Why do you want to live, mein Herr?" Alaric returned the old man's query with bold slyness.

"Because, my boy, there is still much that I wish to accomplish, especially in the field of music," replied the commanding entrepreneur who could tell by the youth's words that his dedication was very strong indeed and this pleased him highly.

"I have only just begun to accomplish the things I want to do in music, so will you please listen to this recording of my song, 'Swan of the Rhine'? Then maybe both of us can accomplish something musically together," suggested Alaric in his seductive pitchman's voice.

"By all means, my boy, let's give it a listen," said Herr Schmidt who was rather tickled by the young singer/songwriter's forthrightness and seriousness.

So the demonstration record, which the youth had record-ed at a Munich record shop, was put on the player in Herr Schmidt's office by his talent scout. The music mogul was quite impressed by what he heard and once the song was finished, he began talking with Herr Klausse about having his charge signed up as a recording artist for Karussell Platte AG.

After much discussion between the two men a contract was drawn up which Herr Klausse duly signed with Alaric because he was a minor. A few days later, the boy said goodbye to his kindly, paternal guardian and darling little sister and went on to become a major recording star.

As the years passed, Alaric Schwan went from world famous popular music star to an executive in the Karussell Platte AG enterprise. So great was the young man's natural business, as well as musical, skill that before long he was the Vice-President of the company and when Herr Schmidt passed away at ninety-three of diabetic complications, Schwan became the President in his place. During this time also, Schwan, who was barely twenty-four at the time, retired Herr Von Fildmann and hired Horst Flugel as the company's new talent scout. As soon as the record busi-ness had changed hands, the little blond pop star turned business tycoon had made it over into an almost exclusively rock-oriented enterprise and expanded it to include a pub-lishing house and a movie studio.

Wise beyond his years, Schwan had been astute to hire the blunt, but brilliant Flugel, for the fellow was to prove him-self to be a great asset over the years to Karussell Platte. This was chiefly because he had, it seemed, a sixth sense when it came to sniffing out new talent. Before long, he and his boss became very close friends and their friendship was to last a lifetime. Three years after Schwan hired Flugel he made him their company's Vice President.

All during this time, Christina had gone from grade school to secondary school to The Munich Police Academy. After graduating from the latter at age twenty, she had hired on as a security guard who protected the lives and property of West Germany's rich and famous. One of her clients was Richard Tag, the tall, suave, blond star of stage and screen. In 1962 he and Christina fell in love and married. They were to remain happily together until an accident in 1967 on a movie set took Richard's life and tore them apart forever.

That was when Alaric Schwan stepped in. He had just organized The Schwagwahr and offered his newly widowed sister a permanent position as the head of it. She accepted and became his heroic and devoted Schagwahr Führerin.

Chapter five

A few years later, with his company well-established and booming, Alaric Schwan and Horst Flugel joined Bavaria's CDU Party and became active in West German politics. While still maintaining the positions of president and vice president, respectively, of their music company, they let a company subordinate handle most of its affairs while they devoted their lives almost exclusively to politics.

It should be noted at this juncture that unlike American politicians, West German politicians were allowed to run businesses without being accused of having "divided interests". All they had to do was make all of their assets public for the situation to be completely legitimate. Luckily, Schwan had never been bashful about showing off his fine, trim assets.

Be that as it may, before long Schwan was CDU party president and when the nationwide elections came, he was elected chancellor by a wide margin. While all of this was going on, Schwan appointed Flugel CDU party vice president and directly following the elections, the new chancellor appointed him president or co-leader of the country. However, Schwan would always have the last word on how the country was to be governed since the position of "president" was largely a ceremonial one in West Germany.

Now on the morning of his fourth day in office, Schwan rose early, as was his custom. Leaving his gorgeous, auburn-haired wife to sleep in a bit in their lavish gold and varnished oak four poster bed with its white satin sheets, flounced canopy, and white and golden-yellow throw pillows, he silently tiptoed out of their bedroom and made his way up to his aviary where he was met by Erik, Erika, Adolf, and Adolfa. Together he and his nieces and nephews fed all of their bird friends. After the last beak was fed its share, the five of them went back downstairs to the dining room where they joined a newly risen "Tante April" and the six other children. By this time his sister, Christina, had joined them and all of the children and adults sat down to eat breakfast in the spirit of happy camaraderie which only a large family can enjoy.

When he was done with his morning meal, Schwan kissed his wife, sister, and the children goodbye and left for his Chancellery in his little white Mercedes. Christina would join him later as the head of his security team, but for the first part of the day, she would have affairs to attend to at Schwagwahrkeep.

As Schwan rode the distance to his office, he forced himself to think on the governmental duties that he would be tackling that day. One of them was a summit conference which he would be holding with the Premier of East Germany. Duty obsessed though he was, his mind could not seem to keep drifting back over and over again to wondering what had actually happened to his twin brother, Atwulf and his Aunt Anna. As he recalled, she had a suitor in the Eastern German city of Leipzig. Wasn't it amazing that the leader of Communist Germany was a man of his same age with the first name of "Atwulf"? Bah! Only a coincidence!, he chastened himself. Then the blond Bundeskanzler, with much effort, returned his thoughts again to office affairs.

While at the office, Schwan spent most of the morning doing routine paperwork. Then 2:00 pm arrived, the hour of his meeting with Premier Atwulf Rotvogel. Sure enough, just as the small fellow had signed the last document, Flugel came bounding into the room.

"The Premier of East Germany is here, Alaric!" he announced in his no-frills manner.

"Good! Show the gentleman in, Horst," said Schwan with a smile. At that moment a visit from just about anyone, even a communist, would have been a welcome diversion from his paperwork which had gotten to be tedious. Besides, he yearned to satisfy his curiosity about the man.

But the second that Herr Rotvogel entered the massive oak door of the Chancellery's main office, Schwan was stunned by the strong resemblance of the East German leader to himself. He had heard rumors of how they shared certain physical features in common and he could see this himself when he saw a photo or news reel of the Premier. Even so, it was not until that moment, while meeting him in the flesh for the first time, that Schwan was able to see how great the resemblance between them really was.

Herr Rotvogel was not only the same height to an inch as Schwan, but had the same light blond hair, boyish features, and intelligent bespectacled blue eyes. Had it not been for his close-cropped haircut, mustache and goatee, plumper physique, old fashioned wire rimmed glasses, and utilitarian dark wool suit, the West German Chancellor would have suspected that he might be looking at his mirror reflection instead of at his guest. He himself was wearing an off-white velvet suit with a ruffled, white silk shirt and his usual aviator-style glasses.

For a split second, the Chancellor stared in bewilderment at the communist premier. Then he quickly regained his composure along with his diplomatic bearings. It was good that he did this for his negotiating partner was already giving him a wry smile which showed how much he enjoyed seeing the capitalist leader's poise waver.

"Welcome, Mr. Premier, gentlemen. Please be seated," said Schwan cheerfully as he led Herr Rotvogel and his small delegation down to the white velvet upholstered chairs which stood in a section of floor lower than the area which held his desk in his spacious office. He called in a few of his own officials and the negotiations with the German communists began.

During this meeting, which lasted for hours and which centered on mostly East-West trade and arms control topics, Herr Rotvogel had displayed the same arrogant and cold demeanor, to Herr Schwan's chagrin, as had other Soviet Bloc leaders whom he had dealings with. But during the between negotiations, get better acquainted walk, which the two German leaders took together in the leaf- strewn grounds of the Chancellery with only a secret service man each to accompany them, the chubby little Premier's manner was very different. As he and Schwan walked along and chatted together in the crisp November late afternoon, he actually held the Chanceller's hand. The more they talked, the more Alaric could see that without his party cronies, and beneath the harsh red husk of his ideology, Rotvogel was a man very much like himself – studious, cultivated, and more than a little ambitious, but still nonetheless intensely hard working and in his own way, sincerely devoted to his country.

This other side of the small, bearded East German started to put Schwan at ease and make him warm to him. So much so that he confided to him his deepest, most heart-felt wish.

"Herr Premier, I've always felt that the split of our country into East and West was an unnatural thing. As a fellow German, you probably feel the same way, don't you?" ventured Schwan in his most gently persuasive voice.

"No, Herr Chancellor, I'm afraid I never have. As my Uncle Hartmut used to say, 'When a people cleave apart and take two separate paths, no longer can they be one,'" as Premier Rotvogel said this he shook his blond head, although his eyes were twinkling.

When he heard the East German mention his "Uncle Hartmut", Schwan quickly lost color. So he had an uncle named Hartmut too!, thought the Chancellor to himself in shock. It had all become too much of a coincidence for him.

"Are you feeling all right, Herr Chancellor?" queried the little premier with a look of genuine concern on his round, boyish face.

"Yes, thank you, I'm all right. It must be that I'm catching cold in the chilly weather that Bonn's been having lately," Schwan replied as he made a great effort to regain his mental equilibrium.

"Then maybe we should go back inside where it's warm, Herr Chancellor," suggested Rotvogel in a voice full of unmistakable warmth.

When Premier Rotvogel left Schwan later that day, he left him with still more unanswered questions.

But these questions were soon to be answered and in the most startling way imaginable. More than a month later and just before Christmas, Schwan received an urgent communique from the East German Embassy.

"Your Aunt Anna is dying in the Friedrich Engels Hospital in Leipzig. She has an important message for you," was the main point of the dispatch.

After reading it, the blond statesman dropped the communique onto his desk and stared at it in stark disbelief.

"So my Aunt Anna didn't die in the air raid!" he blurted out loud to Flugel who had also read the embassy letter.

"Apparently not. And it looks like she's been living behind The Wall all of these years. Sure is a mystery, Alaric," commented his friend with raised eyebrows.

And it was a mystery which the chancellor was more determined then ever to get to the bottom of. So that same day, he left his work behind at the Chancellory and his family behind at Schwanengarten, and with just a handful of aides, made the flight from Bonn to Leipzig in his private, white, silver swan- crested jet.

When he arrived at the East German city, it was starting to snow lightly. Nevertheless, the diminutive statesman was too excited by the prospect of seeing his long-lost beloved Aunt Anna, whom he had imagined to be dead for forty years, to feel the cold as he and his group bounded up the granite steps to the Friedrich Engels Hospital's main door. Asking his entourage, which included a couple of Schwagwahr in their field gray uniforms, brown Hussar busbys, and brown leather jack boots, to wait in the lobby, Herr Schwan followed Dr. Joachim Krone, the glum-faced proprietor of the hospital, to the ward where his aunt lay gravely ill.

"She has stomach cancer and cannot live past today," said the grim-faced, slightly gaunt fellow as he ushered the chancellor through the ward's white door and then left him to have a private reunion with his elderly relative. Dr. Krone had a sadness in his voice which Schwan was hard put to tell if it was due to worry over his aunt or just habit.

This being East Germany, patients like seventy-eight-year-old Anna usually had to share their wards with ten or twelve other patients. But his aunt was no ordinary patient, as Schwan was soon to find out.

The moment he saw his dear aunt looking so old and frail in her crisply clean, white bed, Schwan's heart ached with love and tenderness. He remembered her as a short, sturdy woman with pixie features and flowing blonde hair. But oh, how age, illness, and years of living under communist rule had cruelly wasted her! The Tante Anna that Schwan saw before him now had thinning hair the color of the foam on beer and a pale, wizened face and form. Even her sparkling blue eyes were as dull as pebbles of blue granite. She seemed like a poor little ghost of her former self. But her smile, as Schwan approached her, was alive with great fondness.

"Oh Auntie!" said Schwan gently as he knelt at Anna's bedside and kissed her frail, white, blue-veined hand.

"Alaric, I'm so happy that you survived that terrible air raid and went on to become everything you've become. How is Christina? I heard that she lived through it too," she said in a weak, but loving voice as she stroked his head of shaggy blond hair.

"She did and now she's my number one police boss and the mother of two sets of twins," Schwan told his elderly relative tenderly.

"How wonderful for her, she was always such a lively little thing," remarked Anna as she managed a smile of amusement. Then her tone and facial expression became more serious.

"Alaric, I am so proud of you, so proud of all you've done. And I'm also proud of Atwulf. You see, I didn't want to die before telling you that Premier Atwulf Rotvogel is your twin brother."

This lightening bolt of a revelation made the West German statesman raise his head suddenly and stare in his aunt's rheumy eyes with stupefaction.

"But...but Auntie, how could…?" he asked with a stammer.

"You must know the whole truth now, dear nephew," she answered in a voice that still sounded firm despite the woman's rapidly failing strength. "On the night of the bomber attack, I managed to save your brother by shielding him with my own body. Once the attack was over, I went to find the rest of our family, but they were all dead. I thought you were dead too, Alaric, and I was in too bad a state of shock to really check out your vital signs correctly. Christina also appeared to be dead and all I knew was that I wanted to get away from all that rubble and those torn bodies as quickly as I could. So with Atwulf in hand, I took the nearest train to Leipzig."

"Once we arrived there, I went looking for Gunther Rotvogel. You remember him? He was my suitor then. He died of heart failure a few years ago. Anyway, soon after I arrived in Leipzig, Gunther married me. Both of us were too old to have children of our own, so we adopted Atwulf as our son. How Gunther loved the boy. He always encouraged Atwulf about everything he wanted to do and from the start did everything he could to interest him in his profession as a piano tuner."

"But he also gave you brother something else. You see, I didn't learn this until after we were married, but Gunther was secretly a communist. And heavens, that was a dangerous thing to be during those Hitler years! I certainly didn't approve of your uncle's ideology, your grandfather raised me and my brothers to be Catholics and good patriotic Germans, but I loved him and so I stayed with him. I even helped him by keeping his ideology a secret and not giving him any friction. After the war, we no longer had to be secret about his political affiliations."

"I didn't even protest when my husband began to instill his communist beliefs in our boy, and instill them he did – gently, firmly, and thoroughly. But he was such a good, kind man and a wonderful father otherwise. It was by his encouragement that Atwulf joined the Young Communist League at age ten and the Communist Socialist Unity Party, which runs the eastern half of this poor, chopped-up country, at eighteen. That was the start of a brilliant political career for him and now he's the Premier of East Germany."

"Just think of it, Alaric, two brothers divided from each other by the cruel vicissitudes of war, just like Germany herself was," mused the elderly lady sadly as she brought her lengthy, revealing narrative to a close.

To substantiate it, she had Schwan look at some documents which were laying on her white metal bed table, and which proved, beyond the shadow of a doubt, that what she had just told him was actually true. With a pounding heart, the chancellor fetched the papers and read each one through thoroughly. When he had finished, he looked up, his small fair face looking as though he had just witnessed a Biblical miracle.

"Does Atwulf know all this?" he asked in an awed tone, his mouth still open in surprise.

"Indeed he does, bruder(brother)!" said a familiar voice and Schwan turned around quickly to see the East German leader who had just strode into the hospital room. His short, chubby arms were open in welcome and he was smiling broadly.

"Bruder!" Schwan cried joyously as he ran to embrace him. With that the two siblings, who were back together again after fate had separated them for so long, hugged each other and wept tears of joy. They then went to embrace Anna who smiled while blessing them both before passing away peacefully, happy for having brought about the brotherly reunion.

It only goes without saying that now that they knew the truth about their fraternal relationship, the summits between Schwan and Rotvogel naturally became more regular, more intimate, and more full of good old fashioned gemuetlich-keit, or warmth, friendliness, and good cheer, than there had ever been before. They visited each other's families, for Rotvogel had a wife and one son, spent much time together on hunting trips in The Black Forest, and even enjoyed beer parties together. And yes, every Christmas they would sing,

"Christmas Town" together just as they had when they were four-year-olds, only now their voices were, of course, fully mature – that is, deeper, richer, and mellower.

The only fly in their perfect ointment was the fact that they had to keep the knowledge of their being brothers from the world in general, especially from the Soviets who would have probably exploited it for some devious end. Still frozen deep in The Cold War, the world was not ready yet to accept their blood relationship with all of its geopolitical implications.

In the spring that followed Schwan's happy reunion with Rotvogel, another shadow from his past was to drift back into his life. But this one was to be of a decidedly more sinister nature. It was then, in early 1985, that really weird and unsettling things began to happen.

Schwan and his wife woke up one morning to find the Latin phrase, "Sic semper tyrannis", ("Thus always to tyrants"), scrawled across his dressing table mirror in April's blood red lipstick in the Schwanengarten master bedroom. Two days later, the Chancellor's copper-tressed wife came into that same room at three o'clock in the afternoon to find a pair of emerald earrings she had left on the oaken bed table. Instead she found, to her shock and puzzlement, that someone had laid out a pair of her husband's white silk pajamas on their bed and driven a dagger through them in the area of the heart. Less than a week later, the chancellor had Gaston Le Rue, the Prime Minister of France, as his dinner guest in the Chancellery's impressive, oak-paneled banquet hall. Just as the two leaders began to discuss the pros and cons of closer economic ties between their countries as they dipped into their dessert of chocolate mousse, each one noticed an unsigned letter by his gilded plate. Each leader's expression went from amusement to perplexity as he read the note addressed to him.

"You are a criminal," read Schwan's note, "Prepare to be arrested!"

"A criminal sits beside you. Prepare the handcuffs!" read the one addressed to the French Prime Minister.

At first, Schwan suspected that a prankster might be behind the above- mentioned unpleasant happenings, so he asked Schwagwahrführerin Tag to be on the lookout for any suspicious acting characters who might be lurking about the Chancellery or Schwanengarten. However, she wasn't able to turn up anything.

Then came a month long lull in which nothing untoward happened to Schwan nor to those around him. During that time the chancellor cut the ribbon on a newly built bridge in Bonn, paid a weeklong visit to Rotvogel in East Berlin, and helped legislate a new farming policy. It was a warm April and everything seemed to be going his way again. Herr Schwan felt wonderful and completely in charge of his corner of the world. So much so that he began to relax the security around him. But he was to regret doing this when May came.

On the afternoon of May 1st, Schwan happened to be sitting at his heavy Chancellery desk breathing in the warm, flower-scented breeze which caressed him through an open window and made him wish he could be outside enjoying it instead of being stuck in his office. Suddenly, his spring feverish reverie was intruded upon by a frantic-faced Tag who had come dashing into his office as though she were being pursued by a ghost.

"Alaric!" she exclaimed. "Someone has blown the Video Room in Schwanengarten apart!"

Thoroughly alarmed at the news, Schwan lost no time in leaving his paperwork behind and heading for his private estate with his police boss in her little gray Audi. The Video Room was located in the left upper floor of Schwanengarten, on the side opposite to the little fellow's aviary, and was composed of four walls covered with nothing but TV screens and a swivel chair in the middle. These security cameras showed what was going on in every room of Schwan's mansion and of the Schwagwahrkeep and the grounds around both buildings as well. It held the eyes of Schwanengarten, but now the eyes had been blown from their electronic sockets and lay blackened, shattered, and sightless on the floor. The Schwagwahr who had been on duty at the time of the explosion had barely escaped with his life. As Schwan stared with dismay at the smoking, gutted mass of broken glass, twisted metal, and electric wire entrails, he suddenly began to remember a verse from Goethe's epic poem, Faust.

> "Phantoms and devils on this law agree,
> Where ever they enter in,
> They must go out again;
> Slaves to the last, in the first they are free."

Chapter six

Things were to get even nastier. On the evening after the conflagration in The Video Room, one of the heavy, three-tiered chandeliers which hung over Schwan's dining room table nearly fell on him as he was enjoying supper with his family. Shortly afterwards, the Chancellor came frighteningly close to being bitten in his own white marble, swan-shaped bathtub when an unknown foe introduced a deadly water moccasin snake into the water pipe. During the following week, he was nearly poisoned when someone put highly toxic sodium hydrosulphide in his food and barely escaped being electrocuted by his own public address system.

Tag too came under attack. One night the lovely blonde paramilitary leader was enjoying a shower in the Schwag-wahrkeep's shower room when she was suddenly lunged at by a lanky man in a black leather suit and a black helmet which covered most of his face. She hadn't been able to see much of her assailant though, since he used a sharp sickle he was carrying to pin her face ward to the shower stall's wall. Not daring to scream, she had stood naked and vulnerable with the water from the shower running down her small, shapely body like cold sweat, while her attacker warned her to "Turn against Schwan or face death!" Then he was gone before she could collect her wits and summon help.

That was the last straw for Schwan and his intimates, that and what occurred four nights later. The bundeskanzler's swan-white Mercedes blew up in an incendiary fury just seven seconds before he and his chauffeur were about to enter it! Naturally, this violent explosion left Schwan feeling badly shaken, although he tried hard to appear cool and unflappable afterwards.

The next morning, his loyal Schwagwahrführerin came to his office with news which left him badly shaken.

"Alaric, my Schwagwahr Agents have just found out who our terrorists are. It's our old enemy Auslaugen again. I don't know how he survived that accident back in 1975, but he did and now he's got a KGB-backed group of thugs working under him. Just recently, they set up headquarters in that run-down old Das Paradies Opera House on Vogel Strasse (Bird Street)," explained Tag who was beaming with pride because her agents, working undercover, had finally discovered the identities and location of the people who had been targeting herself, her brother, and his property.

To be sure, Schwan had ordered her to find out who was behind the terrorist war which was being waged against them ever since the conflagration in The Video Room. But her best Schwagwahr personnel had been as unable to trace the identities of the elusive culprits as they had been to prevent further attacks by them. That was, until then, and Tag felt triumphant in the knowledge her agents had just relayed to her.

Schwan, however, did not share his Schwagwahrführerin's elation. Quite the contrary. The moment he heard the mention of the former composer's name he gave a choking sound like a cross between a gasp and a sob. Then in a shaky voice he said these portentous, guilt-ridden words.

"The body they threw between my feet prevents me from walking," Schwan said softly and in a tone that was loaded

64

with his own feelings of vulnerability.

"I guess that's about the size of it, Alaric. Only this 'body' is still very much alive and on a rampage," said Tag sympathetically, although she, with her perfectly military mind was unable to grasp the irony of his statement. "So what action do you want me to take?"

"None yet, Christina. At least not until after I've talked the matter over with my other advisers," he replied as he regained his composure with great effort.

Later that day, Schwan held a meeting with the entire rank and file of his personal staff.

"Ladies and gentlemen," he began, facing them with his best forthright manner. "It appears that Tag has finally found our phantom terrorists. The question is what to do about them. Do any of you have any suggestions?"

"If the terrorists are ghosts, maybe we should call for an exorcist," suggested a rotund, somewhat comical-looking fellow from Bremen half-seriously. His joke provided a much needed lift from the grimness which the subject of the Trugbilder had already cast over their meeting. Everyone laughed, including Schwan. Then the Chancellor continued with his briefing.

"Very good, Shultz. But seriously now, these Trugbilder, as they are called, and their leader, Winsoln Auslaugen, are real people., And they're a real menace too. Right now they're holding out in that ancient Das Paradies Opera House and who knows what they might do next," said Schwan gravely.

"Why not just send the regular police in and clean them all out?" advised a brooding-faced, dark-haired young fellow in a colonel's uniform.

"Oh no, Martin, that wouldn't do at all! These Trugbilder have strong communist connections, and if the police raid them and haul them into court it will look bad for Atwulf and his people. Everyone will think they've been backing them up all this time, even though they haven't," Schwan reminded him.

After listening for an hour or two to his panel of advisers, Schwan decided that the only person who could deal with the problem of Auslaugen and his Trugbilder intelligently was himself and so he dismissed them and made plans to confront the Trugbildführer face-to-face. Because it was a rainy July evening, the diminutive blond fellow drew on a long, white, hooded cloak which was made of water-resistant silk and which was held at his proud, fair throat by a gold, swan-shaped clasp emblazoned with a grape-sized diamond. Because it would be dark inside of the old vacated opera house, which for years had stood ignored and neglected in the Turkish slum area of Bonn, he would bring with him an electric lantern in the shape of an old fashioned coach lantern. As he fingered the skeleton key that undid the padlock and chain which the city had placed on the crumbling building's doors, Schwan laughed to himself over the rumors he had heard about the place being haunted.

"Alaric, you can't go in there alone. There's a dozen crazy, mad bombers running around loose in there," warned Flugel who had insisted on accompanying his Chancellor as he was driven to Vogel Strasse.

"A hundred-dozen probably. But don't worry about me, Horst. I've got my luger pistol with me in my suit pocket," Schwan told him nonchalantly as he pulled his hood over his pale blond hair in an almost flippant gesture.

So Schwan's right-hand man had no other choice than to comply with his wishes and leave him to sit waiting for him on the cracked gray-blue marble steps of Das Paradies as he unlocked the door's rusty padlock. This took some fumbling on Schwan's part since the lock was very rusty indeed and as he worked it, his patience was greatly tested and he wondered how Auslaugen and his cohorts actually made their comings and goings to and from the old art deco- style structure. He could not have known it at the time but the area backstage contained a trapdoor which led to the basement. The basement, in turn, also had a trapdoor and this one led directly to the extensive sewer system that spanned the length of Bonn beneath its streets and tall buildings. It was through this tortuous sewer system that the Trugbilder were able to pull such quick exits and entrances.

Finally, the lock gave way and Schwan opened the two wooden doors with a screech of long-unused hinges that brought an icy chill up and down his short spine. For a second he hesitated. Then he forced himself to go the rest of the way in. But oh, what a creepy and untidy sight met his eyes as he trained the beam of his powerful electric lantern on the ticket office and thereabouts! A lot of the glass had been broken from the windows of the ticket seller's booth and great spider webs spanned their glassless frames. The rain above sounded like phantom foot steps on the roof. Worse than all of this was the thick dust which smothered all surfaces like an ugly dun-colored shroud. In fact, it was so profuse that as Schwan walked cautiously through it on his way from the ticket area to the seating area, he kicked up little clouds of it from the moth-eaten red rug. Treading through this dust layer reminded him of footage he had seen on TV of the Apollo Moon Landing in 1970 which showed American Astronauts kicking up graying clouds of moon dust as they walked and bounded along on the satellite's powdery surface. He started to cough. The building after all had been formally closed since 1954.

Schwan wrapped his cloak tighter about himself for although it was early summer and comparatively warm outside, the inside of the old opera house seemed to reek of damp and chill. As he did so, he made his way uneasily through the seating area. But this section of Das Paradies held even less pleasant surprises for him. He had only taken a step or two through the doorway leading to this sector when a bat suddenly flew past him, nearly causing him to cry out loud and drop his lantern. For a moment, he was really rattled by this happening. Then he got back his nerve and scolded himself saying, "Tut, tut now. It was only a bat," and carried on. However, he still continued to feel very uneasy as he walked swiftly down the dust plagued carpet to the opera house's stage area. In truth, anybody would have felt the same. Now and then the light from his electric lantern spotlighted a rat as it scurried across his path and he could plainly see where other rodents had built nests in the midnight blue velvet upholstery of Das Paradies' once luxurious seats. Occasionally, his battery-powered light would flit briefly over on the round and oval art deco wall frescoes and in the artificial illumination they took on the appearance of...of eyes in the wall!

Alaric steeled himself and finally made it to the wobbly steps leading up to the stage. Once he was up there, he tried not to allow the wide stage's creaky and, in places, weak floor boards to add to his nervousness. Now was the time when his bravery would really be put to the test.

"Winsoln!" he called in a friendly, inviting voice. "I know that you're here somewhere and it's time we talked. I know you feel that I've cruelly wronged you in the past, so let's get together and see what can be done about it."

As Schwan said this, his whole manner appeared to be calm and collected, although he kept his hand in the pocket of his egg shell-white leisure suit's jacket where his loaded luger was and remained on the alert in anticipation that someone or something might suddenly drop to the stage floor behind him. In a moment something – or rather someone – did spring down from the scaffolding above the stage. Only the black-clad apparition appeared in front rather than in back of him. Nevertheless, Auslaugen's entrance was startling and theatrical.

"You little devil, you've stolen my opera, my freedom, my reputation, my health, and my face. But when you stole my country, our country, you went too far. You must be punished severely for that, you dwarf archfiend!" said the Trugbild-führer in a voice full of seething hatred. As he spoke, he towered haughtily over the smaller man, his leather gloved hands resting on his belt where his Red Army issue revolver lay in a holster.

"Yes, Winsoln, I've taken unjust liberties as far as Faustine, yourself, and our country are concerned. But I really want to undo this damage I've done, so I'm inviting you to Schwanengarten where we can write up an agreement about both the governing of West Germany and the staging of your opera which will be agreeable with you. Please Winsoln, we need each other. You can't accomplish your objectives without my money and connections, and I can't do without your genius and fine leadership skills," Schwan said all of this in his most beguilingly persuasive voice, knowing that he had to humor this erratic fellow who was apparently so unbalanced that he thoroughly believed in the violent path he was following.

Even so, Schwan's sales pitch had the effect on Auslaugen that he desired. For the Trugbildführer had heard Metternich-style cunning in the Chancellor's voice, but in this instance Metternich was saying what he wanted him to say.

"Very well, Schwan, I'll go along with this, but if you betray me again, my Trugbilder and I will have your impious little head," Auslaugen told him emphatically, his one icy blue eye glaring down at him contemptuously.

So with that decided, Auslaugen rode with Schwan back to Schwanengarten where the Chancellor took him by a special back door up to his Synthesizer Room. This chamber had walls which were covered with the glittering, flashing control panels of a monstrous Moog synthesizer. Although such electronic musical instruments had by that time become decidedly more compact, Schwan clung to the bulky old music machine out of an almost sentimental attachment. In the center of it all was a heavy Gothic table made of dark oak. The whole atmosphere inside the room seemed to throb with an electric heart beat.

"Winsoln, this is where I go whenever I'm in the mood to compose songs or when I just want to be alone. You know how it must be for me with the huge family I have. Anyway, there's a room adjoining this one with a bed, a bathroom, and a refrigerator full of food. So just make yourself at home here," said Schwan as he attempted to add to his

70

guest's comfort by helping him off with his helmet. The little fellow was soon sorry that he had done this.

"Horrible! But I'll hire the best plastic surgeon in Europe to work on you and you'll be as handsome as ever. In the meantime, let's draw up an agreement and then you can go right to work writing up a new constitution for governing our fair fatherland," offered Schwan whose revulsion at seeing the marred left side of Auslaugen's face and empty eye socket had quickly turned to compassion.

In respect of the Trugbildführer's privacy he gently lowered his helmet back over his heavily scarred face and sat down with him at the oaken table where together they wrote up an agreement in which the Chancellor promised to give most of the powers of governing over to Auslaugen. Auslaugen also made sure that there was a clause included which made null and void the terms of the previous agreement he had signed with Schwan concerning the rights to Faustine. After the whole paper was written up, the two men duly signed it and Ausluagen began working on his new constitution for West Germany.

At this point, Schwan could see that the Trugbildführer wanted to be alone to work on this project and so he left him to do so with the promise he would be back from time to time to see how he was doing or if he needed anything. Already, Auslaugen had become engrossed in drafting this document. So much so that he barely acknowledged it when the one-time Entrepreneur left him. Nor did he hear it when the door of the only exit from The Synthesizer Room was bolted shut with a sharp metallic clang!

Two evenings later, in the Schwanengarten living room, April was busily arranging a bouquet of sweet basil in a delicately carved vase of solid jade. She had just picked the fragrant nosegay from her herb garden and as her dainty pink fingers skillfully arranged the basil into a neat cluster of bluish -white and green, she reflected on how much men were like plants – strong, yet capable of bending, basic, and so "earthy". Her Polish cousin by marriage, Joseph Wabencha, reminded her of the sweet basil. Like it, he was spicy, tantalizing, and poignant. She saw her husband as a plant too. A short, but proud and sturdy linden tree with broad branches. For what could be more truly German than a linden tree?

Suddenly, April's foliage-filled reverie was torn into by a most blood-curdling scream which nearly caused her to drop her vase, sweet basil blossoms and all, on the off-white carpet beneath her. The scream seemed to have come from the kitchen and so, without a further thought, she laid the vase down on a nearby shelf and headed in that direction.

With her children tightly beside her, the mistress of Schwanengarten entered the mansion's huge, well-equipped kitchen where the Chef, Walther Von Ei, and his three assistants, Joachim, Dieter, and Erwin, were busy cooking the evening meal.

"I thought I heard a scream coming from here. Are you gentlemen all right?" she inquired, her beautiful hazel eyes wide with fear and wonder.

"All of us are fine here, Mein Gnadige Frau (My Good Lady), but we did hear a scream too. It probably came from the big parrot upstairs," said the portly Chef with the thin mustache as he stood with his hands on his massive hips. One of these ham-like hands held a soup ladle.

72

His answer seemed to satisfy April who nodded at him and his staff with a relieved smile and then left the kitchen with her children tagging along beside her. Herr Von Ei and helpers had cooking and baking to do. These young cooks and bottle washers, however, had not been so easily assured.

"It must be that ghost again," said Joachim as he rolled out the dough for the noodles that were going to go into the Pilzauflauf mit Nudeln (Baked Mushrooms with Noodles) that the Schwan household had ordered for supper that night.

Joachin, thin and red-haired, was a lad of about seventeen.

"You mean the ghost that's been been poisoning our master's food?" asked Erwin who was plumper and darker than Joachim, but of about the same age. He stopped momentarily in the middle of chopping up parsley to stare at his kitchen mate with great interest.

"Yes, that ghost. A trugbild they called it," said Joachim in a low confidential tone as he fumbled in a kitchen drawer for the noodle slicer.

"That trugbild had to be a ghost in order to slip past the Schwagwahr so easily," joined in Dieter who was stirring chocolate pudding on the stove right across from the two other kitchen boys. Tall and heavyset with blond hair and green eyes, Dieter at twenty-four was considerably older than Erwin or Joachim, although he was nonetheless as superstitious.

"Now stop talking such nonsense, boys, and pay attention to what you're doing or I'll make you eat all of your cooking mistakes. The trugbild was not a real ghost, but a living terrorist and he'll never sneak back in here to poison Herr Schwan's food again, because Herr Schwan has really tightened up security around here. That shriek you heard was probably just a big bird upstairs. Now, get back to work!" said Herr Von Ei with fatherly brusqueness.

Chapter seven

But little did the Chef know how true his words actually were. The piercing shriek had come from a big bird – a big bird named Winsoln Auslaugen. One hour after Schwan had left him in The Synthesizer Room two days earlier, the Trugbildführer had begun to feel hungry. So he left the drafting of his constitution behind and went to the small refrigerator in the adjoining room where he found a half-dozen tart-sized meat pies. He took a bite of one, got a terrible headache, and then blacked out.

When he again returned to consciousness, Auslaugen at first felt groggy, dazed, and physically numb. Then slowly this mental veil lifted and sentience fully returned to him. However, his head still hurt a bit. He picked himself up off the heavy white shag rug which had broken his fall and which covered the whole floor of this room adjacent to Schwan's Synthesizer Room.

It was then that he glanced over at the day clock which told both the time and the date on the white end table beside of the chamber's small, white, ermine fur spread bed and received a shock that jolted him awake completely. He had slept the clock around – not just once but twice! With a new feeling of urgency, he bolted for the door of The Synthesizer Room, only to find it locked tight.

He then threw his helmeted head back and screamed at the very top of his lungs! He screamed in fury, he screamed in frustration, he screamed in anguish, as the full realization that Schwan had locked him up and thrown away the key again hit him mercilessly. When this initial outburst was over, he composed himself and began thinking hard. The first thought that came into his mind was that Schwan had poisoned him and then had sealed him in The Synthesizer Room to expire like Fortunato in Poe's The Cask of Amontillado.

But although all evidences around him seemed to prove the truth of this conclusion, it was not the case. It was not poison in the chicken tart that made him black out for two days but his old head injury and although Schwan had indeed deliberately locked him in The Synthesizer Room, he had done so without any homicidal intentions. Schwan had simply wanted to put Auslaugen in a secure, hidden place until he could discuss him at length with US President Robins. Heaven knows, his actions carried international political connotations of the most crisis provoking nature. Furthermore, Schwan surmised, though wrongly as it turned out, that if the Trugbilder were leaderless, they would be easier to deal with.

As it was, the Chancellor was about at his wit's end in his dealings with his politically charged specter. Many times he had relented and begged the regular police to join his paramilitary Schwagwahr in combating the growing Trugbild terrorist force. But well-armed and brave as they were West Germany's men in blue had proved to be no match for the elusive and Soviet-backed communist force. Worse still, this phantom army had managed to absorb every other West German terrorist group, even the Baader-Meinhof-Gruppe. The Trugbilder were like poltergeists that had declared the country their haunting zone and all other forces, whatever their ideology, had to beware. Both the toppling of the West German Government and possible world war threatened.

"Still, I will not take the life of this maniac if I can help it. Once I discuss the matter with Robins, we will know what to do. And don't think we can't get valuable information out of Auslaugen and then use it to cripple terrorist movements all over Europe. No, I can keep him under lock and key," Schwan had said over the protests of both Tag and Flugel.

Even so, it mattered little to Auslaugen whether his nemesis planned to kill him kill or not. Either way, he was trapped in a place he couldn't get out of. However, he was far from stranded in The Synthesizer Room. For unknown to Schwan, he was carrying a compact high-powered walkie-talkie which he always kept handy along with his pistol. He fished it out of the left bottom pocket of his black leather tunic, switched it on, and made contact with his Trugbild Lieutenant, Dietrich Kierst, who was still in his headquarters with the others in the sub-basement of Das Paradies.

"Come with a detachment, Kierst. Schwan has trapped me in the right- central room in the upper story of Schwanengarten," he ordered.

"Ja, Mein Trugbildführer, right away," replied Lt. Kierst with a mixture of military dutifulness and preciseness.

In less than an hour, a detachment of Trugbilder under Lt. Kierst had gone through the branch of the city storm sewer which lay the closest to Schwanengarten and had emerged from a manhole to grapple with the guards at the estate's elegantly wrought iron gates. Taken by surprise, these Schwagwahr were quickly overcome by the superior numbers of Trugbilder who managed to put them and the gate's heavy lock both out of commission before they could call for reinforcements. The Trugbilder then forced their way through to the Chancellor's mansion where they met with wave after wave of heavily armed Schwagwahr led by Tag. But the Trugbilder were heavily armed also. With machine guns, army rifles, and hand grenades at the ready they were able to break in and free their leader.

As soon as he saw the melee starting, Schwan phoned Hans Von Sperber, the Bonn Chief of Police and frantically asked him to send officers to intervene. Right away, Polizeipräsidet Von Sperber, sent a large swat team which joined the ranks of the Schwagwahr. After a terrific fight, the Trugbilder were successfully routed. Most of them had died along with, apparently, Auslaugen himself. Indeed, the casualties had been very high on both sides. The three red invaders who had survived the fight, out of Lt Kierst's detachment of twenty, were wounded and put in Bonn's high-security federal prison until the little statesman could figure out what to do with them.

From the moment Schwan had seen the clash between the Trugbilder and his Schwagwahr beginning, he had sent April and the children to the lower east end parlor where he judged they would be safest and gave them guards to protect them. He himself had conducted the fight, sometimes right in the field of conflict beside his sister and sometimes from the newly rebuilt Video Room with Flugel.

When the skirmish was finally over, Schwan was convinced that he was rid at last of all his old adversaries, including Auslaugen. He was especially grateful to his Schwagwahrführerin for the role she had played in defending him, their property, and their family from the terrorists.

"My dear, your tactics against those Trugbilder hoodlums were ingenious. And now we're finally rid of them. You deserve a medal for this and a medal you'll get," he told

Tag elatedly as the last Trugbild was taken away in the swat team's squad car. To be sure, the Chancellor was grateful for the help given by the polizei and would find ways to show it, but for him it was Familie Über Alles.

So preparations were made for Schwan to award Tag the Iron Cross First Class in a special public ceremony in the Chancellery auditorium on September 4th at eight pm. As this big day approached, the enormous old hall with its heavy oaken chairs, vaulted wooden ceiling, and velvety wall paper of white and yellow-gold edelweiss design, was given a thorough floor to ceiling cleaning and polishing. Even the chairs were reupholstered and a new carpet was laid down. All of Schwan's closest political associates were invited to this major ceremony as well as the general public.

The program of the medal award gala would call for Schwan to make a speech at the auditorium's massive dark oak speaker's podium. This would be followed by a speech by Tag and then would come the big moment. At precisely eight o'clock pm, Schwan would pin the Iron Cross on the Schwagwahrführerin's ample, uniformed bosom as the orchestra in the pit below the struck up the national anthem "Das Deutschlandlied" followed by David Bowie's "Heroes". A one-thousand dollar plate fundraising supper would then top off the whole affair.

On the morning of September 4th, work personnel draped the whole inside of the Chancellery auditorium with red, yellow, and black tricolor West German flags, and streamers and bunting in the same colors. For the whole week previous, all of Bonn had been buzzing with excitement over the event which was soon to be taking place there.

Unknown to the Bonn populace and certainly to their

Chancellor himself, was the fact that others were busy making plans of their own for the night of September 4th. Schwan truly believed that the Schwagwahr and polizei had disposed of all of the Trugbilder on the night they stormed his mansion and that their leader was dead, for real now. Von Sperber having had Das Paradies checked out from attic to basement seemed to verify this. But they were wrong on both counts, dangerously wrong.

The regular police inspectors had found no Trugbilder in or under Das Paradies simply because they had found a new hiding place and one which the Landeskriminalamt (Police Investigators) and the Schwagwar investigation branch would have least expected – the vaults and tunnels of the labyrinthine sewer system directly under the Chancellery itself. Far from being dead, Auslaugen was with them very much alive and planning something especially nasty to surprise Schwan with when the night of September 4th arrived. What's more, he still had plenty of Trugbilder to help him pull off his last and most desperate stunt, both in the sewer with him and hiding out at Dr. Krane's farm ready to be called in at a moment's notice.

By six o'clock pm, the spacious government building was already packed full to capacity. Anybody who was anybody was there, from West Germany and elsewhere. Schwan's brother, Atwulf Rotvogel, was there sitting up in the balcony with his East German delegation. Auburn-haired April sat in the very front row with Schwan's six children. Nearby them was his French friend and ally, Prime Minister Le Rue and his delegation. In a mezzanine box to the right was US President Robins with his petite blonde wife, Betsy. Even the Soviets had sent a high-ranking envoy.

Auslaugen was there too and standing so close to Schwan

80

that the little fellow would have felt uneasy had he been aware of it. For the Orchestra Conductor who stood below the stage with such expressionless, almost imperious, mien in his neat suit and tails and with his shiny dark brown hair slicked back was none other than the Trugbildführer in disguise. Directly before him were his armed personnel, all hand-picked for their musical ability as well as for their bravery, which formed the orchestra itself. The real forty member orchestra and its Conductor, called the Bonn City Philharmonic, had been waylaid by the Trugbilder and killed by them. They took their clothes, instruments, and IDs, and then hid their bodies in the least frequented region of the Bonn sewer.

Along with the tuxedo, which the Conductor, Hanns Perlmutter, had been wearing, Auslaugen also enhanced his resemblance to the man by putting on a very lifelike wax mask. This mask depicted Herr Perlmutter's features exactly and had been made for the Trugbild leader weeks ago by his surgeon friend, Dr. Krane. Luckily for Auslaugen, he and Herr Perlmutter were of about the same tall, lanky build. He had even decided to wear a glass eye. This would complete his disguise, since the Conductor had also had blue eyes.

At precisely eight o'clock pm, the stage's yellow-gold velvet curtains finally opened and there stood Schwan at the tall, flag-draped speaker's stand, looking handsomer than ever in his off-white velvet suit, ruffly sleeved white silk shirt, and highly polished alligator shoes. In his wide white silk tie was a diamond the size and shape of the ill-fated Hope Diamond. At his right side stood dutiful Tag looking resplendent and Joan of Arcish in her trim field-gray uniform with its heavy gold piping and gleaming brass buttons. On her pretty, but serious blonde head was a Schwagwahr busby emblazoned with a gold German eagle. On her feet were well-polished jackboots with gold riding spurs. At Schwan's left side stood faithful Flugel looking like a peasant in his Sunday best in his brown tweed suit and black and white saddle shoes. In his thick hand was a small red velvet box containing the Iron Cross.

Looking balefully up at his foe, Auslaugen noticed something which only he and his "orchestra" could have seen from their vantage point and which set him to snickering under his wax mask in spite of himself. In order to be chest level with the speaker's podium, little Schwan was forced to stand on a chair.

The audience, most of whom were oblivious to the goings on in the orchestra pit at the time, cheered enthusiastically the moment the curtain lifted on Schwan. He raised a swan-white gloved hand in a gesture commanding silence. As if on cue, they all fell quiet and he began his speech.

In this monologue, which lasted an hour, Schwan eloquently praised his Schwagwahrführerin for her sterling virtues which included bravery, forthrightness, and loyalty. Towards the end of this speech, he even went so far as to say that whenever she defended him, she was defending all of West Germany as well.

Tag, who was an inch shorter than her brother and therefore also needing to raise her stature with a chair, then took the podium and began her own speech. The commanding lady's talk was a brief, but stirring presentation of the dangers of terrorism, of which, she proclaimed, the Trugbilder were the worst possible examples. From there, she went on to stress the urgency of the West German public supporting her and her Schwagwahr so that all such menaces would be defeated and the country would remain a safe place to live.

At the end of each speech, the people in the audience expressed their unconditional support with much clapping, cheering, and stomping. Using diplomatic good taste, both speakers had been careful not to mention their Trugbild enemies communist connections. That revelation would have been compromising to Rotvogel. It would also have been unnecessarily rude to the Soviet envoy.

Now the speeches were done and the big moment had arrived at last. Schwan, Flugel, and Tag took their places in front of the audience with their backs to the speaker's lectern. Flugel handed the box containing the medal to Schwan as the clock in a tower outside struck eight pm in the chilly, dark air.

That was Auslaugen's cue, but instead of raising his conductor's baton and leading his orchestra in playing a rousing rendition of the German national anthem as the program had called for, he quickly threw down his baton, threw off his disguise, and with pistol in hand, stormed the stage with his legions beside him, their machine guns blazing.

The chiming of the clock was also the cue for the Trugbilder in the sewers, who had now been joined by the group from the Krane farm. Rallying together, they had burst out of the manholes at the first strike of eight like maggots from a dead horse's belly and fought their way through the Chancellery to the Auditorium where they quickly laid armed siege. They thus prevented the terrified audience from exiting the room, many of whom were already starting to panic and stampede. To add to their helplessly trapped condition, a Trugbild had even cut every phone line in the Chancellery.

At first the Schwagwahr had been too stunned by the suddenness and audacity of the Trugbild assault to act, but then Tag quickly rallied them to the defense and they began to hit the invaders back with ferocious zeal. A skirmish then resulted of small-war proportions both inside and outside the Chancellery Building.

Meanwhile on the Auditorium stage, Schwan had been knocked down, along with a couple of Schwagwahr who had been standing closest to the stage, by the first volley of fire from the four hundred Trugbilder's machine guns. His off- white suit soaked crimson, he was wounded, but would survive. Flugel had him taken off in an ambulance and then turned his attention to helping get April and the children out to safety. He succeeded in doing this, but before he could make his own escape, a Trugbild grenade knocked a heavy piece of mortar from the wall directly above him. This fell on his head, crushing and killing him instantly. Tag had perished from a bullet from Auslaugen's pistol, but before she died, she had grabbed a machine gun from a fallen Schwagwahr and finished off five Trugbilder in one fell swoop. This done, the gun slipped from her hand and she breathed her last. As she died she regretted that she had not had a chance to kiss her beloved brother one last time.

One of her bullets struck Auslaugen in the chest and as he himself lay dying, he gave one final gasp while looking out over the chaotic panorama of what was to be remembered as one of the most climatic events of the Cold War.

Finis

SWAN OF THE RHINE

Chapter one

Eight-year-old Alaric Schwan loved those hiking trips in the hills with his father, Helmut, his twin brother, Atwulf, and his dachshund, "Abby", Abholen. He especially relished these outings when it was a fine spring day like it was that morning with a warm April breeze wafting through the linden trees and birds of all kinds chirping and calling. Some of them left their perches and flew around, occasionally very close to the human intruders to the delight of both boys. Now and then orioles and robins would settle down to hunt for grubs in the green moss that carpeted the forest floor or in the crevices of a fallen, decaying tree. Now and then Abby would go chasing after a bird, but his short little legs wouldn't let him move fast enough to catch one.

"It smells like spring," remarked Herr Schwan as he led his two tow-headed sons and dog along the woodland path strewn with leaves and small twigs. "This is what the color green smells like too. All of the leaves and moss and old, fallen trees."

"And frogs! They're green too, papa!" said Alaric excitedly as a large bullfrog suddenly leaped across their path.

"Yes, they are, son, and their being out and about is another sure sign that spring is here to stay," said the short, pudgy, blond father between puffs on his wooden pipe.

As he said this his sons and Abby suddenly got the whim to go chasing after the frog. He chuckled as he kept his pace near them while they bounded after the amphibious creature, trying to pounce on it and grab it. Once Alaric thought he had the creature, but it easily slipped out of his fingers and with an almost teasing *croak!* plopped itself in a nearby brook and disappeared under some lily pads.. With Abby scampering behind, the boys returned to the father, disappointed but still enthusiastic about the natural wonders around them. There were more wonders to come. Just then there was a sudden splash of white further down on the same lily garlanded stream.

"Swans!" exclaimed Alaric as he pointed in the direction of the splashing, yet still graceful, commotion. Abby let loose with a round of barking.

Indeed, once the water had settled four pristine white swans could be seen floating in a perfect line, neck to tail.

"They have come to hunt food and then build nests," said Herr Schwan with a smile, thinking with a touch of pride how these graceful waterfowl shared his surname.

"I saw some baby swans once in a book about birds," injected Alaric. They were all fluffy and gray."

"I saw them too and were they ugly. Like in the story, The Ugly Duckling," remarked Atwulf who had glanced through the same book.

"No, baby swans are not ugly!" retorted Alaric who was a serious bird enthusiast.

"They are too! They look the color of mud!" protested

Atwulf who had other ideas.

"Now, Atwulf and Alaric, you're missing the lesson behind that Hans Christian Anderson fairy tale. All birds are beautiful in their own way and if you judge anyone's or anything's worth solely by the way they look on the outside, you miss that beauty on the inside. That's the beauty that counts," Herr Schwan chastised them mildly.

The two boys stopped their bickering and became quiet for a moment. Then they heard a couple of warblers trilling as they perched in a lofty linden nearby, and their boyish glee returned to them. Soon they were chasing each other over and under the crumbling logs and tree stumps with Abby joining in the fun and their father not far behind.

All too soon, the day had come to an end and it was time for them to return to their home in the city. The sky was already pulling down its curtains of yellow and red sunset. First there would be supper and then Alaric would spend the rest of the evening perfecting his piano playing skills and working on a song he was composing. The songs he had heard in the bird calls and the frog ribbets during his hike that Saturday were further inspiration for his songwriting. The boy already knew how to find musical inspiration from the simplest features of life around him.

Indeed, music was Alaric's whole life and had been, it seemed, when he began to talk. That was when his mother, Isolde, first starting giving the boy piano lessons.

"There, that's it. That's how it's done, Alli," blonde, pixie-like Isolde would tell her son coaxingly as she patiently guided his chubby little fingers with her own over her grand piano's ivory and ebony keyboard.

Alaric picked up the skill of piano playing quite fast and at a rate that surprised even his parents who had great faith in his inborn talent. With this expertise, the boy was developing a love of music which seemed much beyond his years. His singing skills were growing very well too, under the coaching of his mother, who had once been a professional music and singing instructor. She was also teaching him how to write music, so when the boy turned five, he delighted everyone with a simple tune about, you guessed it, "A Stroll In The Woods".

The boy would continue writing and playing songs. Then the clouds of war darkened the horizon of his life and his homeland. He lost both his parents in an British air raid, while his brother was carried off by communists to what would one day be East Germany. He endured the spartan hardships of the Nazi system and rose above the indoctrination it tried to force feed him daily. It was not all tragedy, however. In the midst of this strum und blut, a baby sister named Christina was born and eventually a loving distant relative named Emil Klausse took them both into his home and hearth. Herr Klausse bought the boy a grand piano and encouraged him with praise and the coaching from a teacher at a local music academy. With his music, Alaric was able to survive everything the World War threw at him. When Hitler fell and peace come on Europe like a sudden illumination of bright light following a long dark winter, young Alaric's music gave background music to that light.

By then his triple musical talents as a singer/songwriter/musician had matured so fast that he was able to record his first hit single, "Swan of the Rhine", at the age of fourteen and was hired by the prestigious recording company, "Karussell Platte Ag. (Ferris Wheel Records, Inc.) This folk song ballad with slight classical touches was intended to be a paean to his homeland, since the "Swan" of the song's title represented Germany in its gallant, beautiful, high-minded aspects. As such, it was a musical counter thrust against the demonized image that far too many people all over the world now fostered against his beloved fatherland because of the blight of the two ugly ideological twins – first nazism and now, communism. All political considerations aside, "Swan of The Rhine" brought the young boy a small fortune along with considerable early fame worldwide.

While Alaric's family had lovingly, though strongly encouraged him to do well with his musical education, they hadn't let his regular schooling slack off either. When the time came for him to begin attending primary school, his father had enrolled him at Der Eule Schule, Munich's finest grade school. Later on, when he was ready for secondary school, Herr Klausse had seen to it that he gained admittance to the city's widely respected Rabenschwarz Oberschule. As a student, Alaric would not disappoint his family nor his teachers, since his quick mind and eagerness to do well at every task to which he applied himself helped him earn good grades in nearly all of his subjects.

After graduating with top honors from Rabenschwarz, Alaric began to take an interest in the business side of the music industry. So he had Herr Klausse enroll him at the renown Munich School of Business and at the same time kept on with his musical career.

Although Alaric's time was somewhat divided between music stardom and school, he was so scrupulously organized by nature that he managed to do exceptionally well at both. He was such a success with his lessons at Rabenschwarz that he graduated at eighteen on the school's honor roll.

It all paid off in marvelous dividends for the young man with the blond Beatle haircut and stellar voice. When Alaric turned twenty the President of Karussell Platte died of diabetic complications and he took over the position as head of the entire company, – record presses, recording studios, and all!

Chapter two

A bit later on, businessman Alaric Schwan hired short, rotund, sausage-loving Horst Flugel as his talent scout. He first met him as the manager of a little known, but promising rock group called "Der Pinguine". Flugel wanted them to record on Schwan's Karussell Platte record label and was quite forward and skillful in his promotional approach. Along with an audition tape containing some of Der Pinguine's best songs, Flugel sent the Entrepreneur a fourteen inch cardboard box full of air holes which contained a live, New Zealand penguin. This was done as a pun, since "pinguin" is the German word for "penguin".

On top of the bird's box was glued an envelope. Schwan tore it off and opened it. In it was a note that read, "Feed me. I'm yours." and a letter recommending Der Pinquine as star material for Karussell Platte. Both were written by Flugel, who ended his letter with the suggestion that Schwan contact him after he had listened to the audition tape and then made up his mind one way or the other about it. At the very end, he mentioned that he could contact him at Adler Platte, the largest rock record retail outlet in Stingen, which he happened to be the Vice Manager of and which Der Pinguine more or loss used as their headquarters.

Schwan had smiled with amusement as he read the messages. The "feed me" note intrigued and tickled him, as did the main recommendation letter's confident, straight forward tone, the audition tape reel, and the bird itself. As a matter of fact, he felt tickled all the way down to his backbone, a place on him that was hard to stimulate, even by massage or acupuncture. He listened to The Pinquine's audition tape and was pleased by the band's high quality in sound, originality in style, and already polished professionalism. After listening to the cassette all of the way through twice, Schwan felt convinced that Der Pinguine were much more than just another garage band. Right away, he dictated a letter to Dietra Steiglitz, his Secretary, in which he eagerly invited Flugel to bring the rock band and come to his record company office in Munich so they could sign a contract for the group.

"I want your superfine band on my Karussell Platte label. They have what it takes to become a real hit band and I know a potential hit band when I hear one," read one passage of Schwan's letter.

A few days after the Entrepreneur had sent off this letter to Flugel, he spied a sleek, black and white minibus pull into the large parking lot beside of the Karussell Platte Ag. industrial complex. When he saw that an umbrella toting penguin wearing a top hat and bow tie had been painted on both sides of the van he knew for certain that his new soon-to-be stars had arrived. As Schwan continued to watch out of his office's western window, Flugel, cute as a penguin and as chubby as one, stepped briskly out of the minibus wearing a black tuxedo, black top hat, white vest, white gloves, and white oxfords. In his right hand he carried a black closed umbrella for no other reason than for show since it had not even been raining that day. Then all four of the Pinguine piled out of the minibus and followed after him. They all appeared to be skinny, nineteen-year-old youths with neat, but shaggy, long blond hair. The four of them were wearing tight black leather slacks, glittery white shirts, and black leather ankle boots with high heels. Behind them trailed about seven roadies in blue jeans and T-shirts stamped with the same kind of umbrella toting penguin motif that was painted on the minibus. These roadies were carrying all of Der Pinguine's instruments and sound equipment as they followed faithfully at their spiked heels.

Pleased with what he saw, Schwan left the window and sat back down again in his red velvet desk chair. There he waited for his new clients to come to his office. A few minutes passed, and then he heard a feminine voice coming out strongly over the intercom on his office's ebony wood desk announcing that a man who called himself Horst Flugel and who had a rock group called Der Pinguine and a bunch of roadies with him, wanted to see him immediately, if not sooner. It was Fraulein Steiglitz again. Schwan pressed one of the gold buttons on the intercom.

"Great, Dietra, I've been expecting them. Have one of our sound technicians show the roadies where to put their instruments and amplifiers in Gieher Studios and then bring Flugel and his group into my office," Schwan ordered in his mellow voice as he spoke into the intercom's gold wire screened speaker.

"Will do, Mein Herr," replied Fraulein Stieglitz quickly. Before Schwan could reshuffle the stack of papers on his desk, his short, thin, ash blonde Secretary had brought Flugel and the Pinguine into his office. After Flugel finished introducing himself and the members of the rock'n'roll quartet, the Entrepreneur invited them all to sit down in the heavily upholstered chairs that spanned his desk. Stieglitz took a seat close beside Schwan, while the manager and his group seated themselves in the row of chairs facing him. Flugel placed his top hat and umbrella in his lap.

After everyone had seated themselves, Schwan had mused briefly to himself at how the little dark haired man was almost as short as himself and Fraulein Stieglitz, who were five feet two and five feet, respectively. Then he brought his mind back to the deal he hoped to cook up with his guests.

Being the tough, astute businessmen that they both were, Schwan and Flugel wasted no time in getting down to the project at hand, which was signing a contract that would make Der Pinguine part of Karussell Platte Ag. They negotiated for two hours, during which the Pinguine just mostly looked on as spectators and smoked joints. Schwan himself smoked a number of small French cigars in a gold, diamond-studded cigarette holder as he and Flugel talked. Generous host that he was he shared a stogie with the agent who lit it with a ceramic penguin-shaped lighter. The Entrepreneur was impressed by the tenacity, boldness, and far sight with which Flugel tried to get the best possible deal for his band.

This shrewd fellow is one really good manager, thought Schwan as his negotiations with Flugel became increasingly more involved.

Finally, the contract they had been talking over was signed with Fraulein Stieglitz acting as the witness. Der Pinguine would record on Karussell records and do a number of live concert tours with Schwan's full promotion. The record mogul decided to keep the real penguin, which Flugel had sent him, as a personal pet in his growing aviary.

The Pinguine proved to be an even bigger success on the record charts than Schwan had imagined they would be.

Just a week after the group's first single recording, "My Best Memories Are Of You", was put together in Gieher Studios and then pushed to DJs all over the country by Schwan's ambitious promotional department; it began a steady, but sure climb up to the number one slot. This new band was to make several more hit singles that year, and by the
beginning of the next year their first album, "Brenner Pass Train Station", would sell over a million copies and earn a gold record for them.

Schwan realized that these successes of the Pinguine were as much the results of Fugel's managing as the group's talent and his own smart promotional tactics. He admired the firm, but flexible way that he managed them and looked out for their needs in general. The plump little plock-wurst-loving fellow was like a father to the four teenagers who made up the Pinguine rock band even though he was barely older than they were. He made sure that they arrived on time for all of their recording sessions, that they did not get too stoned before an interview, and that they didn't get screwed over by greedy, unscrupulous promoters.

Schwan was so impressed by Flugel's keen sense of responsibility and skill as a manager, as well as the fact that he obviously shared his sixth sense for sniffing out rock star material, that he finally offered him the position of Chief Talent Scout for Karussell Platte Ag. Always eager to get ahead in life, he had accepted the proffered position without any coaxing. Of course, Flugel had given up his job as the Vice Manager of Adler Platte though he would remain the sole Manager of Der Pinguine even in his new capacity. Schwan had been wise indeed to make Flugel his talent scout. For many months and years to come, he was to bring potential new star after potential new star into the electronic domain of Gieher Studio's Audition Room.

In appreciation for his bringing in so many dozens of hit-bound, new artists for him, Schwan gave Flugel several promotions within his company. Before long, he was company Vice President and second only to Schwan himself in authority over Karussell Platte Ag. Not surprisingly, the enterprising Flugel would remain a very important and indispensable figure in Schwan's professional life.

Chapter three

It was not long after the rising success of Der Pinguine began that Alaric Schwan decided it was time for him start looking for a wife. For years he had been followed by legions of panting groupies and female performers, all of whom found him irresistible with his blond good looks and fine voice, not to mention his soaring achievements as a business tycoon. However, he had found all of them shallow and boring once he got to know them. Then too, he was more staid than most and women of their caliber found that discouraging. Because of his strong religious principles, he was able to keep himself from falling into the clutches of both alcohol and narcotics addiction and from dipping into the temptations of sexual licentiousness that flaunted herself all around him. To be sure, during his rock star days, he had dated several girls, many of them top rock stars. He was always careful to keep these dates pristine, however.

Holding hands and a kiss were about all they could expect from the charismatic, but sober young man.

Finally, when he reached his early twenties, the Entrepreneur did meet the love of his life and future bride, but as it usually happens, they met when he wasn't looking for a mate. At the time he was looking for a new star, one that would put his music industry in a fresh new groove, so to speak.

"We need a new artist for our record label, Horst. Someone with a really different, exotic sound," Schwan remarked to Flugel one day as he paced the red shag carpeting of his luxuriously furnished Karussell Platte Ag. Office.

He wore his pale blond hair shoulder length as was the style during that apolitical era of his life and affected a slightly "Carnaby Look" with ruffly shirts and velvet suits with wide bell bottom trousers. Behind his round glasses, which had been especially tinted to double as sunglasses, Schwan's intense blue eyes showed that he was deeply em-broiled in thought as did the set of his small, thin-lipped, but strong, mouth. His fine features also reflected his concern over the way his company was getting stereotyped as an exclusively rock and pop oriented industry. Like any other successful businessman, Schwan wanted to expand his market by appealing to a broader segment of the music-lov-ing population. All the better to increase his sales. Flugel, who was sitting across from him in one of the office's thickly upholstered ebony chairs, shared his boss' concern. He also had a solution to the problem, or believed that he did.

"How about a sitar player, Mein Herr? You can't get any more exotic than that," Flugel ventured.

"What in Saint Micheal's name is a sitar?" asked Schwan as he suddenly stopped his pacing and turned to face his Vice President skeptically.

"It's an oriental instrument a lot like a guitar. It's really popular with the kids these days," replied Flugel who was pleased to discover that he knew something his Entrepre-neur didn't.

"Sounds interesting, Horst. Do you know any talented sitar players we could sign on?" queried Schwan who was be-coming more and more intrigued by Flugel's suggestion.

"I know of one that looks like a good prospect," as Flugel said this he showed Schwan the front page of an American music tabloid called Variety. On it was the picture of a remarkably beautiful young woman with sparkling hazel eyes behind slender-framed "granny glasses", a round, fair complected face, and glossy, reddish-brown hair. She was sitting on a stool and holding in front of her an exotic looking instrument with a long fretted neck and a gourd-shaped body. Over this striking photograph, which seemed to Schwan to radiate an almost lifelike charisma, was the caption, "April Aries, Mother of the Electric Sitar, Now Playing At San Jose's Majestic Theatre With Beatle Tour". Under both caption and photo was a brief description of the sitar player and her career. Schwan took it all in with evident relish.

"Great! Pack your things, Horst, we're going to California to recruit this bright new artist for our record company!" he said with evident delight in his smooth, baritone voice.

The very next day, Schwan and his number one man boarded a private jet and after sixteen hours and a brief stopover in Paris, arrived at San Jose's bustling airport. Feeling exhilarated at the prospect of meeting the obviously talented Miss Aries, the Entrepreneur was whistling Dionne Warwick's hit song, "Do You Know The Way To San Jose", as he and a slightly groggy Flugel grabbed their luggage and hurried out the airport terminal's revolving doors. It was 7:45 pm and April Aries' show was scheduled to begin at eight o'clock pm. From the airport, Schwan and Flugel left in a rented limousine for the bright neon lights of the Majestic Theatre in downtown San Jose. By 7:58 they were in the famous music emporium's spacious lavender and blue halls sipping drinks at a round wooden table which faced the roomy, pale purple curtained stage.

Schwan had, as usual, ordered a cognac, while Flugel had ordered red wine. The place was packed that night and everyone, especially the two Germans, were anxious for April Aries to come on stage. She was to be the first act that evening, that is, the warm-up act for the British pop stars who would be featured later.

Suddenly, the lights of the hall dimmed and the stage curtain went up to reveal a small, fair young woman in a green paisley blouse and matching miniskirt. On her feet were brown leather sandals. She was standing in front of a mike and held an electric sitar in her arms.

"And here, cats and chicks, is the one, the only April Aries! Direct from the Wolverine State!" bellowed the black M.C. as he strode to the stage and introduced the auburn haired girl. In an instant the M.C. was gone and Miss Aries was left alone onstage. With the glare of the footlights beneath her and a revolving mirrored ball scintillating above her, the musician played her sitar with the skill of the best East Indian masters, but with a refreshingly modern, western bit of improvisation. When she sang, her voice had the sweetness and purity of Mary Hopkins, but also the power and hypnotic quality of Grace Slick, the resonant-voiced singer of the rock group which was at that time known as Jefferson Airplane. At times, she could even become strident like Janis Joplin.

All the songs that she did were originals which she had composed herself. One of them included, "For Jim", a rock ballad love song which every DJ in the United States and Canada said was sure to be a hit.

Everyone was enthralled by the fair young lady's performance and gave her a standing ovation after her show. No less captivated was Herr Schwan himself who showed his approval by throwing April Aries the Nineteenth Century gold

Gulden coin which he always kept as a good luck charm. The sitarist picked it up and smiled at the West German record tycoon. Then she bowed and left the stage. Not wanting to stay for The Beatles Concert, which was sure to bring a volcanic uproar from the female members of the audience that Schwan would find it difficult to do business negotiations over, the record magnate left Flugel with his wine and found the M.C. who was nursing a scotch on the rocks at the table closest to the orchestra pit. Handing the man a large roll of American one hundred dollar bills, he explained in nearly perfect English that he wanted to meet April Aries.

"Hey man, I've got to meet this superfine new artist!" he insisted politely.

"Then follow me this way," said the M.C. with casual friendliness as he took Schwan's money and led him backstage where the lady musician was talking with a trio of excited male groupies.

"Wie Gehts, my name is Alaric Schwan. I'm in charge of the Karussell Platte record company and I've been putting great instrumentalists on vinyl for years. But I've never heard anyone play as well as you," Schwan said with a broad smile as he showed the lady his business card.

"Thank you, sir, my talent's not much, but I love what I do," replied April Aries as she shook the businessman's proffered hand. "And you must be the really cute blond guy who threw me the gold coin. Thanks for that too, I like collecting coins in my spare time."

"Ja, it was me. Now can we go someplace and talk privately, Miss Aries?" asked Schwan hopefully.

It was prudent of him to ask this. Now that the main act had taken stage, the noise from the audience was already starting to build.

April Aries, who was intrigued and flattered by the little Entrepreneur's sales pitch, quickly led him to a small table in a comparatively quiet corner near the dressing room section. After both of them were seated, she asked him what his business deal was. Without any more formalities, Schwan laid out his proposition for the singer/songwriter/ musician to record with his company for a considerable sum of money. He presented a contract for her to sign. But Miss Aries wouldn't even look at it until after she had consulted with her plump, middle-aged Agent, the well-known Arnoldo Fenicio. She called him over to join her and Schwan at the little corner table.

It was very necessary that Mr. Fenicio, who came from San Francisco and had a slight Italian accent, be brought into their negotiations. He had been her well-connected and experienced Agent ever since she seriously applied herself to having a musical career. While April Aries and her agent were both intently studying the contract, Schwan left them and a few minutes later returned with Flugel who also managed to find a place for himself at the small table. After several hours of haggling between the four of them, a deal was finally hammered out and Miss Aries signed on to record with Roustabout Records – the Los Angeles-based American subsidiary of Karussell Platte Ag.

After the contract was signed, Schwan and the rest re-turned to his table in the concert room where he ordered dinner for the four of them. Not being able to find any Ger-man food on the menu, Schwan settled for a hamburger steak with mashed potatoes and gravy and another cognac, while Flugel ordered lobster and wine. He would have preferred a plate full of sausages steaming with sauerkraut, since he was an avid lover of his nation's wursts, but that was, as has been already noted, as far from the content of the Majestic's menu as the planet Mars. April Aries and her agent both requested pizza, but while Mr. Fenicio also ordered wine, she asked for a root beer instead as she happened to be underage.

  While The Beatles played in the background and audience screaming erupted all around them, Schwan, Flugel, and their two clients dined. Between bites the two Germans leaned close to Miss Aries so as to hear her better as she began to gave them a few more personal facts about herself, some of which made their eyes widen with amazement. She had been born on April 10th, nineteen years ago which made her nearly five years younger than Schwan who happened to be twenty-three at the time. It was because of her April birth date that she had been given her spring-evoking first name. That was also the origin of her "Aries" stage name, since the days which fall between March 21st and April 19th are said by astrologists to be governed by that zodiacal sign. Her real name, she explained, was April Dawn Berger and her birthplace had been Ann Arbor, Michigan. She was the second daughter of Kenneth Berger, who ran the most lucrative refrigeration business in the state. He was German and had as one of his ancestors, General Hanns Von Berger, a famous Prussian mercenary who fought bravely beside of George Washington's men during the American Revolution. He was also distantly related to Israel Putnam, a General who also fought for the American cause.

  "I'm told that I do resemble General Putnam with my round face," remarked Miss Aries proudly, though half-jokingly. The others laughed. Schwan began to warm towards the girl a great deal more after hearing about her German-American ancestry.

As she nibbled on her pizza, Miss Aries continued her history, explaining that her mother, Doris, on the other hand, was English and proud of it.

"My maternal Great-Grandmother, Nettie, came over on a boat from London with my Great-Uncle Ned. They settled in the thumb area of the state near Bad Axe. She was only fifteen, but could lick her weight in wildcats. She worked in a fish canning factory and later married a businessman, George Averie. He became my maternal Great-Grandfather and Uncle Ned went to work for his business which was ship building," said the girl wistfully.

"Very important industry in Michigan because of all the transport being done on the Great Lakes," added Schwan as he gazed into her hazel eyes with growing admiration.

"And in Hamburg in my fatherland too," injected Flugel who liked to travel about the city of Hamburg and go on boat trips off its piers in the summertime.

"Yes, I've heard of that fine Northern German city. I would like to go there someday and see it myself," said Miss Aries who was starting to really like these new business acquaintances of hers, especially Schwan whom she thought was as brilliant as he was adorable.

She noted that she was at five feet three an inch taller than him. Despite that he came across as larger than life to her.

Returning the blond tycoon's smile, Miss Aries resumed the tale of her early life. She was the youngest of four children. There were two older sisters and one brother. Their names were Debbie, Marsha, and Alex. Right from the start, both parents had made sure that she and her siblings had received the best education and all of the benefits of life. This was especially true in her case since the circumstances of her birth had been very portentous. On the midnight that she was born, a glowing red object had appeared directly over the roof of the hospital where her mother was struggling to give birth to her. As she took her very first gasps of air, the object exploded into two yellow and two orange fireballs and streaked off eastward as though borne on the wings of angels.

Mildly superstitious, both her parents took this to be some kind of divine omen and from the beginning did everything they could to grow her potential.

Because Doris had gone to the Partridge College For Women in Liverpool, England, she insisted that her youngest daughter have the same opportunity. So when April reached sixteen, she was sent off to the British girl's academy.

Chapter four

This move was to be educational for the young lady in ways that were totally unexpected. April had been an avid Beatles fan since her early teens and when she sailed for England to begin her attendance at Partridge, the musical foursome was just starting to get popular outside their own country. While enrolled at the college, she got into trouble with the faculty by frequently leaving the premises without permission to attend concerts put on by the fab four. April eventually even met and made friends with the individual members of the group, especially Paul McCartney, and they all taught her how to play British style pop music. The young Michigan girl had always had a talent for music and from the age of four knew how to play her father's guitar and mandolin. The Beatles helped her perfect her guitar playing skills and taught her how to play the sitar. She proved herself to be unusually talented on both instruments; so talented, in fact, the mop top foursome insisted that she start performing on the same billing with them.

April, who was eager to emulate her English musical mentors, hadn't needed much prodding to join them in rock stardom. Without their having to invite her twice she had taken on her April Aries stage name and grabbed up her guitar and sitar to accompany them in gigs all over England. Not long after April Aries' first concert tour with The Beatles, Paul McCartney, who happened to be the most interested of the four in making custom-made instruments, helped her construct her brainchild – the electric sitar. The teenage girl from Ann Arbor had even recorded a couple of records with his group's own Apple Records company, but she hadn't signed a contract with them because she felt at the time that she just wasn't ready to be tied down to one recording business. Along with The Beatles, April Aries had also become the friend of Welch folk singer, Donovan Leach, whom she counted as the second greatest musical influence in her life after John, Paul, George, and Ringo.

It wasn't long, however, before the staff at the Partridge College For Women finally decided that enough was enough and permanently suspended Miss Aries for her many truancy violations. As it turned out, she had been sneaking out of her upper story dorm room through a window on a rope she made by tying several bed sheets together. Immediately following her suspension, April Aries had moved in with Paul and his first wife, Linda, at their Liverpool home where she was to live for a year or so. The Beatle and his spouse looked out for her as though she was their younger sister. When their first child, Heather was born, Miss Aries took care of her like she was her own beloved niece.

At this point in her discourse, April Aries expressed the sincere hope that her close association, both personally and musically with Sir Paul and the other Beatles could continue despite her newly signed contract with Roustabout Records. Schwan who was a bit of a Beatles admirer himself assured her that it would.

Satisfied with the Entrepreneur's promise, Miss Aries went on to confess that her parents were initially upset with her when they learned of her suspension from Partridge. Even so, when they out how successful she had become as a pop star, they both forgave her and gave her their blessing. Her father especially was both amused and elated.

"Dear, it looks like our daughter has traded the woman's college for the college of musical knowledge," he said with a wry smile to his wife Doris while they were having brunch at their Michigan mansion.

"Indeed, she has. I guess those Beatle guys are smarter than they look. They've not only helped her with her music, they've kept her from falling into the clutches of both cads and greedy record tycoons," agreed the thin auburn-tressed lady.

As she said this, her eyes twinkled even though she was still disappointed over the fact that her youngest daughter had chosen an unexpected career direction. Doris Berger had the most remarkable eyes. They were mostly blue with specks of brown in them. "Buttermilk in my blue cream eyes", she called them.

Their youngest daughter wrote and phoned often even during the seven or so concert tours that she had accompanied The Beatles on since her leaving the woman's institution of higher learning. Often, they came to her shows. They were unable to come to this one, Miss Aries explained, because of a business deal her father was embroiled in at the moment. They had phoned her earlier, however and given her their "best wishes". So had her siblings who had also embarked on their own lives and careers. Alex was studying business at Michigan State University, while Debbie now worked at NASA, and Marsha was happily married and applying herself as a homemaker.

April Aries then ended her summing up of her life to date by explaining that the Beatles tour she was doing right then happened to be her third such tour of the United States. During her first visit stateside as a performer she had met flamboyant, charismatic rock singer and head of The Doors rock group, Jim Morrison. They had sung a duet together and he had been so taken by her that he had invited her to be his lover. She had kindly declined however. Her parents had raised her to be cautious about sexual encounters and her family's Methodist faith kept her from falling into that dangerous trap. After all, what kind of secure love could such a rider on the storm and wild child, no matter how charming, have been able to offer her? How different was the stable and staid Alaric Schwan. She could already feel a healthy chemistry between them brewing.

Before the evening of their first meeting was through, April Aries and the West German tycoon had grown very fond of each other and a close friendship was born together with a new career upswing for both of them.

"May I call you Al, short for Alaric," ventured Miss Aries to Schwan one afternoon while both of them were taking a coffee break after a particularly hard recording session at the Roustabout Records recording studio.

"Only if you let me call you, Prili. My pet name for the month of your birthday which is in my heart the least cruel of months," replied Schwan as he smiled fondly at his lovely companion. His own birthday was August 21st .

"My dear friend, it would be an honor for you to call me that," said April Aries with the most deeply felt sincerity. As she spoke, she placed her dainty, though strong hand on the German's shoulder in a sisterly way.

As the businessman and the recording artist continued to work together they inevitably grew closer, since their personalities complimented each other so well. Miss Aries appealed to Schwan because his somewhat dour personality craved the sunshine of the young American girl's sunny disposition, while she saw the German as a highly likable challenge – she enjoyed trying to joke him out of his serious moods and nearly always succeeded.

For over a year, Schwan stayed with his Roustabout Records subsidiary in the United States and nurtured Miss Aries' career as though it was something rare and precious. He let Flugel have complete charge of his company's main branch in West Germany and devoted his time and money to helping her become a great star. Before long, Schwan had gotten "The Mother of the Electric Sitar" signed up to perform at Hurrah's, a posh Las Vegas night club, and also at a succession of music halls all over Europe. This was only to be the beginning of a whole series of influential and financially profitable concert tours in which Miss Aries would be the star performer and not just an added attraction. Her first 45 single, "For Jim", peaked to number one on America's top 40 music charts as was predicted and stayed there for several months.

In the months to come, this hit single would be followed by three more, the last one being a jivy instrumental titled "Signal!". Miss Aries would also record two albums which would reach gold status, that is, sell over a million copies, within just a few months. The initial album, Electric Paisley Scarf, was a collection of all of the young girl sitarist's hit songs to date, plus five new previously unrecorded tunes. The cover of Electric Paisley Scarf featured a striking portrait of Miss Aries done in psychedelic dayglo colors in which she was wearing a green paisley dress and the squarish sunglasses which were to become her trademark. These darkened shades had lenses that also helped with her near-sighted condition.

The second album, which featured all new material, had a photographic cover that depicted the musician sitting knees up in the sand wearing a blue jean skirt and sandals and wrapped up in a blue blanket with white swan motif. Nearby, the azure waves of the Rhine River were rushing and rolling. Her sitar was slung across her strong, lovely back. Quite rightly, this album was titled River Songs. Soon after this long playing record was released, Schwan, with the help of some friends in Hollywood, produced one of the rock music industry's first so- called "rock videos" with April Aries as the star performer. This fifteen minute minimovie showed the lovely sitarist in a tight, flesh-colored body suit taking on a whole number of sensuous poses against a solid black backdrop, while a galaxy of multi-hued neon city lights flashed superimposed across her shapely form and her own melodious voice sang the dramatic rock tune, "Crazy Mad For You", in the background. This pioneer music video was to add to Miss Aries' growing fame in America and all over the world and sparked talk of a possible movie career for her in the near future. Indeed she was soon given the lead role in the West German romantic drama film, "A Shower of Lilacs" and played the part well which involved a lot of singing as well as acting. As it was, Miss Aries made the film a huge success in Europe.

Her relationship with her Entrepreneur had continued to grow as well. In between music tours and his tasks and responsibilities as the head of his record corporation, the sitarist and her promoter dated. Then came the blissful day that they were so sure of their feelings for one another, that Herr Schwan proposed marriage to Miss Aries and she consented. In December of that same year, she became Mrs. Alaric Schwan and returned with him to West Germany. Without regret April Schwan gave up her musical and acting career and her husband left a trusted executive in charge of

Roustabout Records while resuming direct control of Karussell Platte Ag. They were to have six children.

Chapter five

After ten years of being a music industry tycoon, Alaric Schwan decided to leave the music industry and embark on a political career. So he left his entire conglomerate in Herr Flugel's, faithful, capable hands and went on to prepare for this new vocation at Bavaria's scholastically formidable Falke Universitat.

As has already been noted, although he had devoted most of his youth and early adulthood to a musical career, Schwan had also managed to gain a thorough education in other areas. Therefore, he was not to enter the doors of the major university unprepared. Then too, because he had done so well at the renown Munich School of Business, the towheaded little man was certainly no stranger to higher education. However, he had never before attended a university of the stature of Falke Universitat before and so it was with some calm apprehension mixed with determination that Schwan approached its well- groomed confines one bright spring day in 1978.

Falke Universitat was a stolid, modern edifice built in the late 1940s of salvaged red brick. It had been constructed from the ruins left by the Allied bombers of World War Two who daily had plied their death-dealing blows to Munich and it environs. The university itself was a long, box-like structure with many wings spreading out from it to form a courtyard.

Its beautiful landscaping more than made up for the plainness of the building itself. Quiet pathways leading through well-tended flowers and shrubs ended, for those willing to follow the flagstone walks, in secluded shady nooks where benches rewarded those seeking peaceful seclusion. Students and faculty alike sought these verdant hideaways – for study, enjoying a snack, or even as a trysting place for lovers. Under nearly every tree in early summer there bloomed a fragrant blue carpet of hardy violets. This delightful display of lawns and natural scenery had been produced by the skilled art of the college's horticulture students who were being taught landscaping by a competent and ardent professor. The ten acres surrounding Falke Universitat were all a credit to this man, a Rhinelander named Bernt Blume, and his devoted pupils.

Spring seemed evident everywhere in the wealth of blooming bulbs and early shrubs which hedged the campus buildings and perfumed the air. The sweet scent of the hyacinths and lilies of the valley wafted on the warm breeze which ruffled Schwan's fine hair softly as he left his red Volkswagon Kafer (Beetle) in the university parking lot and hurried to the registration office.

Schwan now sported a pale-blond version of the early Beatles mop top now that he was grooming himself for a political role and had dropped his ruffly carnaby look for the dark collarless suits with straight, narrow trousers, and ankle length boots originally worn by the fab four. Indeed, this look fit because it was more conservative in aspect compared to the one he presented in his record mogul days and conservative was what he truly wanted to be in keeping with his catholic upbringing. To further show his religious solidarity, he wore a silver cross on a chain. To help with his myopia, he wore photogray aviator style glasses which added to a look of polished professionalism.

   The university department he was headed for was situated in the center of the main building past a waiting area arranged with comfortable seats and a long bulletin board which lined a portion of the left wall. A stairway to the left led up to the second floor and underneath the stairway, the cafeteria fitted snugly against the back wall where the view of the busy courtyard entertained the lunch goer. At the right of the entrance extended the waiting area. From that area forward administration offices loomed ahead. These included the Deans' Offices and Schwan's goal – the Registration Office.

   After he had reported to the Registration Office, Schwan still had quite a few minutes to spare before his first class of the day began. So he made his way to the university's book store which lay just inside the glass doors of the building's right wing. In the brief hallway leading to the book store stood two vending machines – one containing salted peanuts, the other, small, round, sugar-coated chocolate candies. Never a person who could resist sweets, Schwan had procured a handful of them on his way into the book store where he would purchase his textbooks and other school supplies. He also planned on buying an engagement pocket calendar, all the better to keep his tasks at home and on campus in order since he was, by nature, a very organized person.

   When he had made his purchases, Schwan left the book store and walked past a large, round, sunken garden which lay underneath a skylight and was surrounded by benches – a terrarium in miniature. This red brick structure stood to the right of the on-campus shop. On the other side of this sunken garden stretched the learning institution's extensive library – a huge department containing over a 100,000 or so books. The little Bavarian glanced briefly through its glass paneled walls knowing that he would frequent it many times.

Satisfied as to the library's precise location, Schwan turned around and headed out towards the courtyard at the back of the building. As he walked through this wide corridor, he heard the wind moaning softly through it and the sound amused him. On a lark, he began whistling the 1970 Beatles tune, "Let It Be", as though he were trying to counter its melancholy tones with a song that matched the lightness of his own spirits that morning. Wistfully he began thinking of his lovely wife April and began whistling another Beatles standard, "Love Me Do". He would see her for supper later on after all his classes were done for the day.

Minutes later, Schwan was in the courtyard where he found the stairs which would lead him up to room 320 where his Political Science Class would be held shortly. It was 8:55 am and he was still five minutes early.

As he entered the classroom, Herr Schwan nodded a greeting to the other students and the Political Science Professor who were all mostly punctual Germans like himself and who, therefore, had arrived for class ahead of schedule also. His new Professor was a medium stature, Wendish-looking fellow in his late forties named Rudolf Bloch. Prof. Bloch had a ready smile and an oval face which was framed by closely cropped brown hair and a mustache. He greeted each student in an amicable manner as, one by one, they seated themselves at their desks before him.

Under this Professor's guidance, Schwan would learn statecrafting from the bottom up.

Chapter six

So Alaric Schwan pooled all of his mental powers into his studies at Falke Universitat. His courses in Political Science and Law were a fascinating challenge to him and before long, he had learned enough about both subjects to have been able to take his country's governing and judicial bodies apart and put them back together again had he so wished. He also took English Language since he knew that in the role of leader he would be entering the field of diplomacy.

In the process of gaining this knowledge, Schwan began to discover the full measure of his political talent. He also found that the same managerial skills he had gleaned from his years at the Munich School of Business were necessary in running a government. While taking part in class debating teams and running for on-campus elections, Schwan learned too that the charisma, smooth confident manner, and beguiling voice that had won him audiences as a rock star were invaluable assets in winning people over in the political arena. Twice he was elected Fraternity President.

During his third year at Falke Universitat, Herr Schwan became an active member of the Bavarian branch of the conservative CDU (Christian Democratic Union of Germany) Party. He took this step on the advice of Flugel whose father was a CDU functionary in good standing and who belonged to the party himself. Schwan then began to divide his time between his activities at the university and his activities at the district CDU. The latter mostly involved taking part in fund- raising drives and using leaflets and posters to promote the CDU Candidates who included Flugel's own father,

Wolfgang. April, being the supporting and politically aware person that she was joined the CDU Party herself and began balancing her own schedules between being a mother and homemaker and working in tandem with her husband on his political agenda.

Under the tutelage of politically well-experienced Wolfgang Flugel, whose shock of gray hair had once been fiery red, Schwan soon worked his way up to helping work out campaign schedules and doing the loads of paperwork which are part and parcel of a growing governing career. This paperwork was mostly comprised of looking over balloting results and assisting in drawing up campaign budgets. Such basic clerical party tasks might have seemed agonizingly boring to anyone without an interest in politics, but the energetic little towheaded man tackled each one with uncommon zeal powered by genuine faith in his destiny to succeed in a governmental role. While preparing himself for this role, Schwan was obviously enjoying every minute of it.

Schwan continued his courses of study at Falke Universitat and at the end of eight years graduated with Master's Degrees in Law, Political Science, and English Language. He included the latter because English was the tongue spoken the most in diplomatic circles at the time, replacing French which in past centuries was known as the "language of diplomacy".

With a full education now behind him, the diminutive student prinz who was by that time thirty-six years of age, decided that he was finally ready to enter West German politics as a CDU Party candidate.

Around this same time, Schwan's cantankerous grandfather who was a shipping magnate, obliged him by dropping dead at the age of ninety-seven living him the Schwan family fortune of many millions of dollars. Although Alaric still had ill feelings toward the old man, he almost forgave him when the estate was settled and he fell heir to this prodigious sum of money which would go a long ways in financing his soon-to-be political career.

With his inheritance to fortify him, along with his record company earnings, Schwan bought a gothic-style mansion in Bonn's better residential district and moved his family into it. He also took on a pedigreed male dachshund whom he named Kaiser Bill. The little dog was fated to become the mascot of Schwan's CDU Party.

Kaiser Bill's master was now prepared to take the first steps in establishing himself himself as a political leader.

Because his country was one in which elder statesmen of seventy years were still very much revered, Schwan knew that his relative youth would be a score against him. But this would be only a slight handicap since he already had political knowledge and skills that were way beyond his years. What he still lacked was experience and finesse; two qualities that he was astute enough to realize he could only gain through participating directly in the governmental process and preferably in the bottom most ranks of governing. So as part of this on the job training, he ran for positions in the Bonn City Council and was elected twice. Later on, he ran for the office of Burgermeister or Mayor of Bonn and became the youngest men ever to be elected to that position.

Having his friend, Flugel, as his Campaign Manager proved to be a most valuable asset to Schwan not only because of his father's influence within the CDU Party, but because of Flugel's own political and managerial expertise.

Luckily, the stout, sausage gourmand, could handle both their business and a political career besides.

Along this same line, a major cultural difference between West Germany and the United States should be noted. In West Germany, a politician could own a business without it being considered a "conflict of interest" situation. All West German politicians who owned companies had to do was declare each and every one of their assets and everything was considered fair and square. Upright as well as bright, Schwan had declared those of Karussell Platte Ag and all of its subsidiaries before even running for City Council.

At first glance, it might seem a bit hard to believe that a small blond man with a kewpie doll cute face which made him look far younger than he actually was and a pre-political background as a rock'n'roll star could possibly appeal to anyone old enough to vote. Indeed, that was the first impression most of the capitol city's citizenry had of Schwan when he first entered the city's political circuit.

But they would flock to his CDU rallies out of curiosity to see the "odd little mop top" standing at a mike or flag-draped speaker's podium in a park or public building, depending on where the rally was being held, and wonder just what sort of speech was going to come out of him. Then when he began his address there would be something in the set of his chin, in the glint of his intense bespectacled blue eyes, and in the air of command that exuded from his small form and seductive voice that made them see beyond his diminutive stature.

When Schwan spoke of the need for improving Bonn's infrastructure or of the need for progress in a city long held back by political stagnation and then asked for his audience's support in bringing these changes about, they listened enthralled, then applauded, then voted for him.

Very soon, he was elected CDU Party President with Flugel as his Vice President. At this point, both of their political careers became so involved that they turned the management of their record company conglomerate over to Schwan's nephew, Dieter, who was now twenty.

One of Schwan's special assets was his ability to appeal to all age groups within the Bonn populace. For the benefit of the older segment, with whom results counted more than charisma, he backed up his campaign promises with solid proof that he could bring about the improvements that they wanted and needed. If a street required mending, Schwan made sure that it got mended and with the least amount of delay.

Schwan's captivation of the younger voters was a most natural thing because of his own youth and his rock star past. They also backed him for more practical reasons. One of these was his conviction that the ending of unemployment had to be given priority over all other social concerns.

Schwan could also appeal to younger and older generations of Bonn citizens in more theatrical ways too. Besides having his own personal charisma and skills as an orator to draw on, he also used music groups to warm up his audience before he came on the speaker's stand. He would provide a rock band when trying to win over a youthful crowd or an oom pah band if the potential voters happened to belong to a more mature set. More often he would bring in musicians who could play both styles of music well.

It is little wonder that after one of Schwan's political conventions was held in a given district, that people of all ages would turn out in large numbers to join the CDU Party and vote for him. Because of his zealous campaigning and ability to back up his promises with real results, CDU Party membership began to grow by leaps and bounds. Before long it had outgrown the formerly dominant CSU, (Christian Social Union) Party, not only in Bonn, but throughout the Land, or State, of North Rhine-Westphalia where the city is situated.

This development made Franz Hinkel, who held sway as the Ministerpräsident, or Governor, of North Rhine-Westphalia, very nervous since he also happened to be the Party President of the CSU Partei. A tall, burly Nuremburger whose ruddy, fleshy face clearly reflected his forceful, power- grasping nature, Ministerpräsident Hinkel saw Schwan as a formidable political rival and frequently locked horns with the ambitious little man.

Even so, Schwan's position as a politician was secure and both of them knew it. It was therefore with much confidence that Schwan entered his second tenure as the efficient Mayor of Bonn with eyes still on the ultimate prize of the Chancellorship. It was at this stage of the political game that he made his ambitions to win this position publicly known. This announcement was especially timely, since the Federal Elections were by that time only a year and a half away. It was also during this midpoint in Schwan's governmental career that he came to the attention of the brilliant, temperamental ex-Chancellor and former Party President of the CDU Partei, Erich Vogel. Herr Vogel was to prove himself to be, along with the Flugel father and son duo, one of his most valuable and influential friends.

Chapter seven

The friendship between Schwan and Vogel began when the former rock mogul received a blue envelope one day with the emblem of the City of Hamburg – three white towers on a red shield – stamped on it. He saw, to his surprise that it was from former Chancellor Vogel who lived in semi-retirement in that populous seaport city. Upon opening the envelope with a gold-plated letter opener, Schwan found a letter written on blue paper in darker blue ink. It smelled strongly of Old Spice – the cologne of seafarers. Schwan opened the blue letter eagerly and read it. In it, Vogel invited him to come and visit him at his home in the Barmbek district of Hamburg at any time it would be convenient for him. "And be sure to bring your lovely dutiful wife, April," said the missive as an added flourish at the end.

With a smile, Schwan placed the Old Spice-scented letter back in its envelope and then called on his desk intercom for Dietra Stieglitz, who had followed him as his personal Secretary from his record company office to his Mayor's office. Half a minute later, Stieglitz had taken her place by her boss' ebony desk.

"What do you wish, Mein Burgermeister?" Fraulein Stieglitz asked him with an eager to serve smile.

"Please take a letter, Dietra," Schwan commanded mildly and then began to dictate a reply to Vogel.

In this letter Schwan politely specified that Vogel could expect him and April to arrive at his house at 11:07 am on the up and coming Sunday.

Before making the 232 mile trip to Hamburg, the blond Mayor had dressed like a typical Hamburger boating enthusiast in a navy blue fisherman's cap, a yachting jacket, and wide legged sailor's trousers, knowing how much such apparel appealed to his host who always dressed that way himself. April, always the carefree spirit, would wear a billowy blouse with a sailor's collar, a navy blue skirt, a little ribbon banded sailor's cap, and navy blue slippers. Both of them were anxious to meet Vogel and wanted to make the best possible impression on him. This was especially so because they knew that with Vogel to back Schwan up he could go just about anywhere politically, since the elder statesman's words still carried a great deal of weight in the Bundestag, or West German Parliament.

That Sunday, 11:07 arrived with Schwan's new golden-yellow Mercedes Benz touring car pulling into the driveway of Vogel's blue and white, steep-roofed house, following a very uneventful trip. After Vogel's pretty young wife, Alicia, had shown Schwan and April into his cozy, nautically furnished office, the retired politician greeted them with a smile of sincere friendliness on his still handsome, squarish face. As they were being welcomed, the couple had glanced briefly at the walls which were covered with navigational maps and shelves made from ship's rudders. Here and there were crossed boat paddles and sharp harpoons. This ocean theme dominated the entire house and made them feel calm and restful, putting them in mind of Charles E. Carryl's whimsical dreamlike song, "A Capital Ship", in which a wind-blown bedroom becomes a frigate. Suddenly, the couple's reverie was broken by Vogel's penetrating voice.

"Wie geht es Ihnen, Burgermeister and Frau Schwan?" ("How are you, Mayor and Mrs. Schwan?") Vogel asked the blond fellow and his wife as he pumped each each one's hand vigorously. Then he introduced his wife who shook their hands as well.

For a man in his late sixties, Vogel had an exceptionally strong grasp which he had probably earned from years of trimming sails and hoisting anchors. After Schwan and April had returned his and Alicia's greetings, he invited them to make themselves comfortable in two of the thickly upholstered, round backed captain's chairs that stood at attention in front of his heavy plank wood desk which had obviously once belonged to the cabin of some nineteenth century sea captain. His wife took her place in a padded chair which had been made from a ship's barrel. When his guests had seated themselves, Vogel offered the Mayor a cigar from an ocean blue lacquered box with tiny mother of pearl seagulls inlaid on it's cover and sides. Schwan took a cigar gladly and beamed as Vogel lit it for him with his cigarette lighter which had the Three White Towers of Hamburg embossed on it. Vogel did not partake of the cigars, but instead lifted a finely carved ivory pipe from its wooden holder and lit it. Within moments, the puffs from both the pipe and the cigar had filled the room with the rich dark aroma of tobacco.

"I'm going to bring coffee and some crab cakes," announced Alicia with a grin as she left for the kitchen.

"Thank you, Alicia, crab cakes would be a delicious snack," agreed April.

"I didn't know you liked seafood, sweetheart," said Schwan teasingly. He was hungry for a snack himself and on a day like that and in the surroundings that he happened to be nothing could have appealed to his taste buds better.

"I like it now and then. Remember the shrimp salads I always make in the summer?" remarked April with a grin.

"Yes, I do. And I always eat my fill of them. Summer wouldn't be summer without those delectable salads of yours," said Schwan between puffs on his cigar.

"For me going clamming is what makes summer a fine season," added Vogel who was hungry for the crab cakes himself. "We should all do that together on an outing next summer."

"I would like that very much. I used to go digging clams when I was a kid living in Michigan," said April wistfully.

Just then Alicia returned with the coffee and crab cakes on a blue Dresden china tray which she laid on a nearby small table. With the steaming beverage were china decanters full of sugar and cream. Everyone thanked her as she returned to her seat and then partook of the refreshments. Schwan took his coffee with lots of sugar and cream, while the others took theirs straight. Vogel took a long drag on his pipe and then proposed an interesting question.

"Why do you want to be Chancellor, Herr Schwan?" he asked.

"Why did you, Herr Vogel, want to be Chancellor?" inquired Schwan, slyly throwing the question back at him.

"Because our country needed me to make many improvements, especially economic ones," replied Vogel earnestly as he took another long inhale on his pipe.

"Our country still needs a lot of fixing up and I feel that I am just the man to do it," Schwan told him with cool self-confidence.

"I feel that you are too, Herr Schwan. So I am going to give you all of the backing and resources you will need to reach the position of Chancellor. Will you accept my support?" asked Vogel as he stared across at Schwan with the pale blue eyes of a visionary.

"Of course, you've always been my political ideal, Herr Vogel," answered the little blond man with a smile of gratitude.

Following their meeting, which lasted a full hour and their two wives excused themselves from to go for a walk and talk in Alicia's autumn garden, Vogel invited his guests to stay and eat a light lunch with him and his family. His family included six young daughters and the sea-loving fellow introduced Schwan and April to all of them. His guests were charmed by the troop of young ladies who curtsied when they said "Hello". By that time, Schwan was quite hungry as was April. So he agreed that they would stay and join in on the repast. This lunch, which Vogel said grace over, was a bounteous seaman's meal of fillet sole, rye bread, and more coffee, this time spiked with brandy. All of this food had been prepared by Alicia herself and served on the petite hausfrau's blue and white china dinner service on which painted seagulls swooped and soared. After Schwan and April had eaten their fill, they thanked their host and hostess for their generous hospitality and then walked out into a day as gray and as wind borne as the sea gulls that flew in the overcast sky above them.

But Schwan would be back again many times. During their first meeting, a powerful bond had already begun to form between the old ex-Chancellor and the young Burgermeister, a bond which was based as much on personal need as political ambition. Vogel, though sixty-five, was not old for a West German politician. However, a vote of no confidence and a severe case of hyperthyroidism had robbed him of the position of Chancellor after having run the West German Government capably and conscientiously for nine years.

Vogel's thyroid condition had done much to devastate his manly frame. Formerly a husky javelin thrower and weekend sailor, he became prone to nervous fits of the most debilitating character. Then too, the affliction turned his thick brown hair silver-white and gave his handsome, Teutonic features a pale, drawn look. Vogel knew that he was too ill to ever compete again in the front lines of West German politics. Be that as it may, Vogel still had strong views on how his country should be managed and he saw in Schwan a possible means of perpetuating these views and putting them back into practice.

There is also no doubt that Vogel saw in Schwan the son that he had always wanted but never could have had. His first wife, Hannalorre, had only been able to give him one child, a daughter named Susanna, before being fatally stricken with cancer of the womb. His second wife, though perfectly healthy, had borne him only daughters. While in Schwan's mind Vogel seemed to fill the role of his long dead, but still dearly beloved, father as well as his political patron.

It was natural then that Vogel used his still far-reaching influence in government to help his young friend wherever and whenever he could and the two men became very close personal friends. Their friendship in turn added to the strength of the CDU Partei. As the West German national elections drew nearer, Vogel guided his young protege' through the often stormy sea of West German politics with the same fond firmness that he steered his boat, Die Seefluge. He helped him plan his campaigns and made sure that he met all of the right people. He also coached him on how to give his image as a politician more expertise and finesse. The two men became almost inseparable and were often seen in public together dressed in matching navy blue Hamburger seaman's caps and jackets. Schwan even had a rock video made at this time which depicted him and his older, medium statured benefactor thus dressed and strolling through the colorful streets and docksides of Hamburg to the tune of "Three White Towers", a disco-style rock ballad which Schwan had written in praise of the harbor city.

"Three white towers,
Of maritime powers,
Three white towers;
Thru' the centuries these towers shall stand,
All the waters 'neath them to command,
Someday ev'ry one shall understand,
The beauty of these towers above this land;
Three white towers,
Of maritime powers,
Three white towers;
They brood like sentinels o'er river free,
Promising to all security,
So long as they stand shall freedom be,

And Hanse safe from foreign decree;
Three white towers,
Of maritime powers,
Three white towers;
Like beacons of truth they reflect,
The lights of each church and discotheque,

From a shield of red they thus direct,
The glow of fair Hanse so perfect."

The "Hanse" that Schwan referred to in this melody happened to be the northern region of his country in which Hamburg lay dead center.

Schwan and Vogel were frequently seen out boating together with their wives in Hamburg's waterways and many times posed for campaign photos beside of the impressive ships which stood anchored in its long harbor. Once in fun, Schwan had himself photographed lying languidly inside of a large upright ship's wheel.

"Ich bin ein Hamburger!" (I am also a Hamburger!") he would often tell Vogel as he half-jokingly reaffirmed his solidarity with him.

"Ah, Frikedeli." would be his friend's inevitable reply. "Frikedeli" is the German word for the kind of "hamburgers" served in fast food places.

As the time before the elections became a matter of months and then finally weeks, the camaraderie between Schwan and Vogel became more involved along with their campaigning. Whenever Schwan would go out on campaign fund raising drives the elder politician would usually lend a hand.

While in between campaign projects, Schwan was also devoting a lot of his time to building up his own paramilitary force. From the beginning of his career as the head of Karassell Platte Ag., he had always had a well-organized group of guards whose duty it was to protect him, his family, and his private residence, along with the grounds, offices, factories, and various other departments of his business. He gave them the name of Der Schwagwahr, whose name roughly translated meant "Schwan's Army". They in turn were divided up into three separate groups. These were Der Mostru, a condensed version of the term, Motorcycle Storm Troopers. This name was more than appropriate, since most of the youths who made up this force were recruited from biker gangs. They had the job of defending the whole of Karussell Platte Ag. from industrial sabotage and other mayhem. Then there was Der MEST or Motorcycle Elite Storm Troopers whose only duty was to guard Schwan, his wife, and children. Lastly, there was Der SGG or Schwan's Secret Service who were the company spies. These three divisions all wore similar bizarre uniforms which were made up of a tight orlon jumpsuit and gloves and boots of vinyl. But while the Schwagwahr and MEST wore spiked steel helmets much like the kind that were worn by Kaiser Wilhelm's troopers, the SGG wore three layer "energy dome" caps. The main thing that distinguished the three groups from one another in appearance was the difference in the color of their uniforms. MEST wore gray, while the Schwagwahr wore blue gray, and the SGG wore solid black. All carried knives, handguns, iron knuckles, and other such weaponry. Now that he was on his way to political prominence, Schwan was enlarging these private paramilitary forces and secretly giving them bigger and better weapons. He placed his widowed sister, Christina Tag, over them as the commander or Schwagwahrführer answerable only to him.

Before long, Schwan would add another branch to his growing paramilitary forces. This was to be an elite group which would be modeled on the Death's Head Hussars of the early 1900s. At first glance, the massing of personal armies such as these might seem to suggest that there was something predatory, if not outright militaristic in Schwan's nature. However, in view of the fact that terrorism was rampant in Western Europe at the time, especially against politicians at all levels, the small blond man was justified in gathering to himself all of the protectors he could trust and hire.

With his MEST Guards in tow, whom he usually had dress in civilian clothes whenever he went out campaigning so that their presence wouldn't intimidate his voters nor make him seem inaccessible to them, Schwan continued stump-ing vigorously for his ultimate goal – the office of Chancellor. When the West German Federal Elections finally arrived his hard work, coupled with Vogel's, April's, and Flugel's as-sistance, paid off and he was elected Chancellor by a wide majority.

FINIS

THE SWANLING

Chapter one

It was a sweltering evening in August 1945 and German Opera Diva Dorothea Klaussen was taking an in-between performances break back stage at the opera house in Hiroshima, Japan. Perspiring heavily in the lavish black and red brocade ballgown and black ringlet-tiered wig in which she had sung the title role in Leonard Peters' "The Damnation of Christina", she peeled down to her lace slip in her silk draped dressing room and turned on the fan on her triple mirrored vanity. Letting its breezes waft through her wealth of deep auburn curls, she thought of how she was being well-received that night and, despite of The War, she had attracted a huge audience. They had come to hear her sing the part of a beautiful Sixteenth Century German courtesan who had sold her soul and those of her many lovers to the Devil for eternal beauty and political influence. The Japanese opera-going public had loved her as "Madame Butterfly" and they had loved her as "Aida". Now they were loving the fair, petite, blue-eyed songstress with the nightingale voice in the role of "Christina".

It had been because of her popularity in the Asian land that she had risked the bombs and bullets of the Allied Forces and made the rocky flight with her opera troupe all the way from Mittenwald, Germany to this Japanese coastal city. Like all opera singers, Dorothea was multilingual and it had been very expeditious that she knew the Japanese Language as well as her own.

As she continued to bask in the gentle currents of her electric fan, Dorothea thought of her quiet, but brilliant, little tow-headed husband, Max, whom she had left behind in Germany. During the six months they had been apart, their nation had been defeated and brought under Allied Occupation. But, Dorothea had faith that Max Schwanlied and his Schwanlied Ag. entertainment and electronics firm were managing to survive. He was that kind of person.

Dorothea first met Max Schwanlied in 1940 when her career as an opera diva was already at its stellar greatest. Both of them were back stage at Berlin's finest opera house, Die Majestätisch, on that cool breezed, starlet evening in October when the Entrepreneur of the establishment, Karl Von Richter, introduced the future couple to each other during a break between dress rehearsals for a production of Arrigo Boito's "Mefistofele". Because Max loved the opera a great deal and because it was his wealthy Schwanlied Ag. firm which supplied most of the sound and lighting equipment for Germany's music halls and theaters, he was frequently going in and out of the finest opera houses.

Dorothea and Max took an immediate liking to each other and, right away, they started going everywhere together. A year later, their mutual love was stronger than ever and so they married. Dorothea insisted on keeping her maiden name since she wanted to continue performing under the billing of Dorothea Klaussen. Max agreed to let her do this, since any name she called herself by would have been fine with him.

"I don't care what you call yourself, darling. Just don't forget to call me hubby," said the little bespectacled businessman with a fond smile.

Their age difference was considerable. At the time of their meeting Dorothea was twenty years old, while Max was way past thirty. Even so, their marriage began happily enough. Dorothea semi-retired from her opera career, that is, she contracted to perform only when she wanted to, and went to live with her new husband in his light gray, Gothic style mansion home in the Bavarian Alps. They would have a very harmonious home life together, in spite of their being of opposite temperaments. Dorothea was light-hearted, while Max's sense of humor was dry. She was adventuresome, while he was a homebody. She was extroverted, while he was friendly, but introverted. He was quiet, while she was ebullient. But if anything, these very differences in person-ality made them compliment each other and balance each other out. Dorothea liked to tell her friends, jokingly, that she was like a helium balloon and that Max was like an anchor that kept her from "sailing off into outer space". How she missed him.

Just then a gentle rap on her dressing room door and the cheerful voice of Mikiko Heishi, her maid, broke into Doro-thea's reverie.

"Would Madame like some iced tea?" asked the girl.

"Of course, Miki," answered Dorothea as she turned her face away from the fan's breezy caress. "Please bring it right in." She was eager for the refreshment of the cold tea and the girl's blithe companionship.

A moment later, the door opened and nineteen-year-old Mikiko came in bearing a black lacquered tray on which a delicate china tea service rested. She was wearing a col-orful red flowered kimono and a bright smile on her pretty round face.

"I made jasmine tea for you," said the girl as she laid the tray down on a very low cherry wood table that stood in the center of the Diva's dressing room.

"My favorite!" exclaimed Dorothea, clapping her hands with glee.

She sat down Japanese style, that is on her knees, on one of the floor cushions beside the little table. Her maid did the same and then poured some of the cool refreshing beverage into her small porcelain cup from a dainty tea pot glazed all over with painted flowers and cranes.

The two women chatted merrily as they enjoyed their tea and tried hard to put the horrors of The War, that was raging and encroaching ever nearer with each passing day, out of their minds, if only for a few moments. Dorothea deeply admired her Japanese friend's Zen principle of living in the moment, and although she happened to be Catholic rather than Buddhist herself, did her best to live by it.

Just as Dorothea and Mikiko were sipping their second cup of tea, the familiar chimes sounded, alerting the singer it was time for her to return to the stage.

"Uh, oh," said the opera star, "time for me to go back on." Hurriedly and with Mikiko's help, she climbed into another costume, a black, corseted, and broad- skirted outing in the country style dress this time. She put on her wig, touched up her make-up, and swept onto the stage with all of the graceful hauteur of a queen.

It was Act Three in which Christina presides over a May Eve witches' sabbath on top of the legendary Hartz Mountain.

"Witches gather round and dance, heed my call to dance and prance!" sang out Dorothea with truly bewitching sweetness and clarity as a motley crowd collected around her and began to wheel and cavort with impish frenzy. Some were dressed in hooded black robes, some wore the tattered garb of peasants, and some were costumed as nymphs and satyrs.

The whole cast, including the Diva herself, were singing in German for even though the opera had been written in English by an English composer, the temper of the times was such that they wouldn't have dared sing the featured opera in its composer's mother tongue. After all, their country, Germany, and their host country, Japan, had been and in the case of Japan, still was at war with the two major English speaking countries – the United States and Britain. War always brings strange prejudices.

Suddenly, a sound like a mournful wail blasted into the scene of devilish gaiety. It was an air raid warning! Moments later, the whole building shook and a rumble louder and more ominous than a hundred thunder claps sounded.

Dorothea ducked under a prop shaped like a mountain crevice as shrill pandemonium broke out in the opera house. Then the whole world seemed to crumble and tumble down around her and she fainted.

Chapter Two

Hours later, Dorothea awoke in the crisp white bed of a makeshift tent hospital unit. All around her were the sounds of people crying and groaning.

"Mikiko, where are you?" she murmured weakly, her first conscious thoughts being of concern for her friend.

"Take it easy and just relax," said a gray-haired nurse quietly. "Your friend is no longer suffering."

"But is Mikiko Heishi all right?" asked Dorothea anxiously. There was something in the nurse's tone of voice and choice of words that made the Diva suspect the worst.

"I'm sorry, Madam Klaussen, your maid is dead. The air-raid wardens found her lying under the wreckage of the opera house along with three thousand other people. They found you there too and you were one of the twenty that survived," replied the nurse, who was trying to bring Dorothea the bad news gently.

"But that was no regular air-raid, was it?" ventured Dorothea.

"No, we've never seen anything like it before. Whatever the Yankees dropped on us last night flattened our city in one blow. People are coming in here with the worst burns I've ever seen and I've been a nurse for twenty-five years. There seems to be something unhealthy, something poisonous lingering in the air," said the nurse with a look of concern.

Dorothea buried her face in her pillow and wept. Then she thought of Max back in war-torn, defeated Germany and made up her mind to return to him as soon as, and by any means, possible.

Because the Hiroshima Opera House had been many miles away from ground zero, and because she had miraculously suffered nothing worse than shock and a few bruises when shock waves from the nuclear attack flattened the four-story building, Dorothea was able to check out of the hospital unit a few hours later that day. The resourceful Diva, who had gotten her own piloting license when she was eighteen-years-old, contacted the nearest small plane rental agency. She hired a little white and blue two-seater with white cranes painted on its fuselage and climbed into it for a rough trip over the Pacific and Indian Oceans to the Near East and then on to Germany. On the seat behind her was a pretty, black lacquered, Japanese box with a lead lining and a small basket of food and other supplies. At her long, slender, fair throat was an ivory swan pendant – a gift to her from her Entrepreneur husband. She kissed it, said a prayer, started the engine, and was off down the runway. A few moments later, she was off on an uncertain air voyage.

Uncertain it certainly was! All along her flight path, Dorothea ran into blustery winds and battles between Japanese Zeros and US Mustangs. Once she was fired on by one of Chennault's Flying Tigers who mistook her little plane for a Japanese spy plane. At another time, she barely escaped being struck by lightening. During the harrowing week-long flight, she made two fuel stops, one on the still Japanese-occupied island of Luzon in the Philippines, the other in Iran.

When her plane touched down in that arid land's desert plains, the natives had stared in momentary amazement as a white woman in a khaki skirt and blouse emerged from it and came walking towards them asking, in fluent Persian, where she might be able to come by some water and airplane fuel. At first, the three Bedouins who observed her landing, and who happened to be the lookout party for their tribe, contemplated kidnapping her. Then the luger pistol in her belt and the glint in her blue eyes made them think twice about it. So they helped her tank up and fuel up instead and then wished her a blessed flight home.

"May Allah bless you, good lady, and the husband who waits for you," said the leader, a tall handsome fellow with a trim beard, as Dorothea boarded her little aircraft. She called out a "Thank you!" to him and his companions and then was off on the last leg of her adventure.

Three days later, Dorothea flew into Germany. Of course, she was immediately spotted by the radar screens of the US Armed Forces, who were now occupying the country. They didn't fire on her, however, but forced her to land at their newly established airbase at Rosenheim where officers questioned her for hours until they were sure that the mysterious aviatrix was no one more sinister than Dorothea Klaussen, the famous opera soprano. When the questioning was done, one of the US officers, a young Army lieutenant with a carrot red crew cut, smiled at Dorothea and motioned with his head towards the door.

"Miss Klaussen, there's somebody here to see you," he said, his tone changing from an inquiring one to a friendly one. Dorothea, who was starting to feel irritated and antsy because of all the questioning she had been subjected to, tapped her foot and wondered what was coming next.

Just then, the door opened and in came her dapper, tow-headed little husband, escorted by an MP Officer.

"Max!" she squealed with glee as she ran into his open arms.

"Oh, Dotti!" said Max as he smiled and hugged his pretty, spirited wife tenderly. "I've been so worried about you."

"And I was worried about me too, darling, especially when that storm hit near Guam. I don't know what was worse, the lightening or the bombers," she bubbled.

"Thank God, you're back home safe with me here where The War is over," said Max as he kissed Dorothea lightly on the lips, his eyes becoming moist behind his wire rimmed glasses.

"A-hem!" broke in the young lieutenant, as he glanced first at the joyful couple and then towards the door. "You folks are free to leave now."

So Max and Dorothea shook hands with him and the officer who had been his partner in the questioning session, and then left the US Military Intelligence quonset hut building for Max Schwanlied's black and silver Mercedes. He opened the door for her, climbed into the driver's seat, and then they were off.

He drove her through Rosenheim and on to their hometown of Mittenwald, past blackened broken buildings, cracked roads, abandoned shot up motor vehicles, and all of the other detritus of war and defeat which had not yet been cleared away.

Before long, they were in the lofty, clear air-caressed mountains where very few marks of war marred the land-scape. Then they arrived at their gray stone mansion home which was standing as solidly and as majestically as it had for centuries of Schwanlied generations. Once they were settled in its roomy, marble walls, Dorothea showed Max the contents of her black, lacquered, Japanese box and the eyes started out of his head!

Chapter three

As they enjoyed a supper of konigsberger klops (German style meat balls in gravy) and potato salad, followed by a desert of chocolate cake at their long oaken dinner table, Max and Dorothea shared their separate adventures with each other. The couple had a lot of catching up to do. They, after all, had been apart from each other for six whole months and events during that time had been earthshaking for both of them.

The delicious meal they were dining on as they chatted was prepared and served by their beloved housekeeper, Sarah Rabenmann. Pretty, sweet- natured, sixteen-year-old Sarah was a Jewish girl whom Max and Dorothea had snatched away from a group of people who were being lined up to board a train headed for the horrific Majdanek Concentration Camp in Nazi-occupied Poland. During the reign of Hitler, whom both of them had hated but were not in a position to openly oppose, they had kept the girl carefully hidden in a secret chamber of their mansion's vast upper story which was only accessible through a hidden trap door. In this hiding place, which was a true, nicely furnished apartment rather than a shabby, cramped cell or garret, the couple had made sure that Sarah's every need was well provided for and they had only allowed her out of it when they were absolutely sure there were no Gestapo lurking about. Now that the Nazi dragon had been slain, Sarah with the laughing brown eyes and long black hair could come and go as she pleased, much to her benefactor's and her own relief. However, she had decided to stay with the Schwanlied because she loved them and she loved cooking for them, just as she had enjoyed putting together the supper she was eating with them that night.

Since she was like an adopted daughter rather than a servant to Max and Dorothea, Sarah had been eating all of her meals at their white silk draped table ever since it had been safe for her to do so.

"That was quite an adventure you had, Mama Dotti. However did you get past all of the air battles that were going on over there?" the girl asked with widened brown eyes.

"Sheer luck and knowing a bit about piloting," replied Dorothea with a laugh.

Then her tone turned serious. "But you and Papa were having your own adventures. You having to hide for your life and him trying to hold his business together as best he could. So how has Schwan Ag. been doing since I left?"

"It's still standing," said Max smiling.

"Was there any bomb damage?" continued Dorothea.

"Only to the left wing of the record factory. The other buildings were left intact," reported Max with a grateful look.

The very next morning, Max took his wife to the outskirts of Mittenwald where his business still stood. As he gave her a tour of the offices, publishing house, recording studios, electronics lab, and bomb shattered record factory that comprised Schwanlied Ag., he explained that despite the war and defeat the business had continued to operate, though at a slower rate than before. As it was, he had been only to just barely break even and had needed to use his private cache of gold to make needed investments, since the German Reichsmark had died with Hitler.

"We'll need to get more money from somewhere in order to repair all of that damage to the record factory," said Max as he pointed to the broken bricks, twisted metal, and splintered glass of the factory's left section.

"We'll get it," said the determined Dorothea, "and I'll help you! I've still got my voice!"

For the next three years, the Diva worked hard to earn money that would supplement her husband's profits. She toured tirelessly, and not just at opera houses. She wasn't too proud to sing popular songs at nightclubs, beer halls, or US Army canteens. She even began to recruit new singers and musicians for Max to record and promote.

Before long, the damage to their record factory was repaired and Schwanlied Ag. was back in the black again. It was then, however, that the lovely singer started to slow down. Every day she felt sicker and sicker and it soon became a real effort for her to perform. Then she started losing hair and weight and coughing up blood.

"Radiation sickness. You caught it in Hiroshima and it's been growing inside you all of these years," was the verdict of Dr. Taubenschlag, her family doctor.

"Very well," said Dorothea, fighting back her tears. "I will make what remains of my life a testimony."

And make a testimony she did – of the fact that nuclear power when put to peaceful uses must be handled with great care and caution and that it must never again be put to warfare uses. To further this new crusade, Dorothea gave up her musical career and used whatever stamina that remained in her to give lectures, write books, and write newspaper and magazine articles warning against the misuse of the atom.

"Playing with nuclear power is playing with fire and it is a kind of fire that doesn't merely burn you but leaves you with a poison that is always fatal," she would caution with a conviction born of experience.

Dorothea even wrote a poem on the subject titled, "The Deadliest Mushroom."

> "The deadliest mushroom of them all,
> Grows not in the forest where wild birds call,
> But rises up when the A-bombs fall;
> Beware the deadly mushroom!
>
> The deadliest mushroom of them all,
> Before whom the death cup's poisons pall,
> Whose radioactive venom makes strong men fall;
> Beware the deadly mushroom!
>
> Oh world leaders great and small,
> Please heed my warning call,
> And use the atom with care or not at all.
> Beware the deadly mushroom!"

This poem was published in a major German news magazine along with a condensed, though complementary, biographical article about the author.

Her faithful and genteel husband supported her one hundred percent in her new career as an advocate for the peaceful uses of atomic energy only.

"My wife knows what she's talking about. She's been through all the torments of Hell ever since she was caught in that Hiroshima bombing," Max would always tell people with heartfelt earnestness.

As Dorothea's physical strength continued to rapidly drain from her body, Max was all the more gentle, attentive, and patient with her. He would frequently take time out from his business duties to help look after her every day needs. Never was his love for her more strong or tender.

Then in the warm, balmy days of August 1949 Dorothea informed Max that she was expecting a child. Nevertheless, in spite of her increasingly frail physical condition, she seemed optimistic, almost joyous.

"I will have this child and when she is grown she will carry on with my warnings about nuclear weapons," Dorothea said to Max in a profoundly prophetic tone.

The former Diva's conviction was strong that though she herself was likely to pass away, her coming baby would continue on in her place. This sustained her through the months as her pregnancy progressed and her health further deteriorated.

Then on the evening of April 3, 1950, her infant's due date finally arrived and she was taken from her sick bed in her mountain mansion to the maternity ward of Mittenwald's Storchrute Hospital. There she lay gamely enduring ten hours of exceedingly difficult labor.

While Dorothea pushed and strained through her birth pains, the night air outside of the warm, soft confines of Storchrute was murky and chilly. Both the sky and the cool wind were restless, for slender streaks of lightening could be seen probing the grayish white heavens like neon fingers, while the trees were bowed like wizened arthritic crones, their branches and leaves whipping forward with each damp gust like long disheveled hair. The gloom stricken countryside of Mittenwald resounded with thunder which rolled across the darkened forested hills like the beat of a military drum. The moon hid as if in dismay behind her cloak of off-white clouds. Still no rain came.

As the 8:30 pm sky churned and heaved with the forewarnings of a threatened storm, Dorothea Klaussen, at long last birthed the beautiful girlchild she had somehow anticipated. Weak as she was, the poor woman was only able to complete the birthing with the direct intervention of the doctors and nurses who hovered about her, the pristine whiteness of their uniforms almost blinding to her in the overhead florescent lights.

Her girl baby, though listless, was still very much alive and responded weakly when one of the doctors worked to revive her. There was obviously something very wrong with her lungs, so she was handed to a slender blonde nurse who placed her in an incubator. Within a few minutes of being in that oxygen rich, controlled environment, her vital signs began to improve steadily. The infant was going to live.

While all of this was happening around her, Dorothea's own life force continued to drain from her at an alarming rate. Knowing she could not live much longer, another nurse, a plump redheaded young woman named Heidi, was sent to bring her family in from the Waiting Lounge. When her family came to her bed with their faces wet with tears she saw them through mist-filled eyes. Her beloved Max was there among them and he had cut short the closing of a business deal in West Berlin so he could be by her deathbed. Sarah who was still shaking and sobbing was there too. Both of them held her hands.

Then with great effort, Dorothea pulled herself away from the sheer edge of death and sitting up she pointed a pale finger at Max. In a voice which was little more than a whisper, she wheezed, "Max,...give...the...child...the...box!"

This last effort at communication took everything out of her. With a sigh she fell back dead.

Chapter four

Dorothea and Max's girlchild continued to gain strength in the Storchrute Hospital incubator. Her condition was no longer serious, though she remained and would always remain quiet and subdued for a newborn. She slept most of the time and cried hardly at all. Her appetite was poor.

Several hours after her birth, Max held his daughter for the first time. He tenderly stroked her fine golden curls. With muted delight he told Klara Poetzl, the stocky, brown haired, maternity ward head nurse who had just given her to him, "Why, she is as lovely as Helen of Troy must have been!"

Nurse Poetzl agreed.

The little girl was so like the Queen of Ancient Greek legend who hatched out of a swan's egg and whose peerless beauty put men to sword. An adorable, cuddly bundle of pink pearl and blonde, she was already irresistible, especially to the opposite sex. All of the male nurses and doctors wanted to hold and talk to her, whether they were part of the maternity ward staff or not. Seeing a real charmer in the embryo, Max named his child Hellene.

Max was doubtlessly relieved that little Hellene had survived her own birth despite her feeble condition. She seemed every inch the perfect miracle baby. But the doctors and nurses who cared for Hellene before, during, and after her birth know how deceiving her outward appearance really was. Knowing that something was amiss with certain of her internal organs, they subjected the tiny infant to a series of physical examinations. Their suspicions were soon confirmed, for in the course of these tests they discovered that Hellene had been born with only one lung and a heart whose pulmonary artery was blocked. She also completely lacked a pituitary gland. But on the plus side, her intelligence and learning abilities were, if anything, far above normal.

Understandably, the medical staff wanted to follow-up their initial examinations of Hellene with treatments and further tests. They felt that Max should be informed of his child's condition right away since he was her father and they needed his permission to continue with their diagnosis of her. Which was why Dr. Franz Ente, Storchrute's head pediatrician, told Head Nurse Poetzl to bring him to his office immediately after being given his daughter. A stout man with graying blond hair and intelligent kindly blue eyes, Dr. Ente was a man long on experience who knew that Hellene would need special care in order to grow up normally. Max, smiling with relief though his eyes were moist from crying, entered Dr. Ente's office. He was holding his beautiful daughter in his arms, while Mrs. Poetzl stood beside him with her almost unlined face reflecting her concern.

"Good day, Herr Schwan, I am so sorry about the loss of your wife. Won't you please sit down?" Dr. Ente invited warmly.

Max and the head nurse both settled down into two of the large, sparkling white office's ecru, corduroy upholstered chairs. For a moment, Max glanced at the water color prints of Audubon originals which hung in egg shell white ceramic frames on the smooth white plaster walls, each of which depicted a different kind of bird. Then he returned his attention

151

to Dr. Ente.

"Thank you, my good doctor. I know that you and your staff did everything you could for her, just as you are now doing everything you can for my lovely daughter," said Max who was truly grateful.

"You are very welcome, Herr Schwanlied. But I'm afraid our work is far from over. I need to talk with you about your new daughter's health. She was born with some potentially serious, but treatable deformities.

Max's pale blue eyes widened in disbelief at these words.

"But, she's...she's perfect! Look at her!" As he made this retort, he gently held up Hellene before the doctor's face.

Looking Max straight in the eyes with seriousness and compassion, Dr. Ente continued, "You have one of the most beautiful baby girls I've ever seen and she's very bright too. The whole hospital staff and I can vouch for that. What makes her case so sad is that underneath her sugar and spice charm and her quickness to learn she has a few major, internal birth defects, particularly involving her heart, lungs, and pituitary. But, I repeat, although these inner mal-formations are of a very critical nature they are, as far as we can tell, treatable and repairable if we can just get at them in time."

Beginning to finally grasp the seriousness of the situation, Max looked hard at Dr. Franz Ente and asked tensely, "What can I do?"

Dr. Ente returned Max's stare, but in an empathetic manner and answered his query in an affable voice which carried an undertone of urgency, "Herr Schwan, I suggest that you bring your daughter back to this hospital for periodic tests and examinations, say once or twice a week. I could have Fraulein Reiher, the receptionist, set up an appointment for the child at your earliest convenience."

Having shaken his initial startled reaction, Max consented in an amiable tone. "Agreed." he said smiling. Then he and Dr. Ente both stood up and shook hands. With a good natured "Farewell", Max with his newborn child in his arms walked out of the office with Nurse Poetzl who would help him fill out Hellene's birth certificate.

Faithful father that he was, Max kept his promise to the good doctor. After all, he had already lost his dear wife, so he was determined at all costs not to lose his daughter.

Therefore, at Max's insistence, the infant girl began a series of complicated and costly operations and therapies which were to take up her whole childhood and early teens, but which saved her life and insured that she would lead a more normal and healthy life later on. The artery transplants, the pituitary replacement medicines, the biopsies – Max had been eager to pay for it all, even when such treatments had to be arranged for Hellene in America and elsewhere. This was sometimes required because the facilities at Storchrute had been made less than adequate due to shortages and damages brought on by the World War.

It was because of his deep love for his sweet daughter and not just because he was an enormously wealthy business tycoon that Max believed money was no object in his efforts to save her life and health. Had he been themost destitute pauper he would have still found a way to get the money necessary to pay for her treatments.

Then too, the little Entrepreneur sincerely believed that God had a great mission for Hellene to fulfill someday. Every evening that she was away in the hospital, he would pray about her and then look over the contents of the black lacquered Japanese box her mother had bequeathed her.

This became an important ritual for Max, which he would begin by lighting a white candle in a shrine he had set up in his wife's honor in the bedroom they once shared. This candle was set up on a small black velvet draped dais that elevated it a few inches on the shrine. Above this candle was a beautiful painted portrait of Dorothea dressed in the medieval gown she wore when she sang the part of Gretchen in Charles Gounod's epic opera, *Faust*. While below it was the keeper of sacred secrets – the black lacquered box! After lighting the candle with a solemn prayer to the Holy Virgin, Max would take the small chest and gently open it's varnished lid. Any angels hovering over his shoulder saw just why the ill-fated Diva had a special lead lining built into it. For there laying in its red velvet padded interior were six objects with a tragic history and a poisonous taint – an irradiated rock, a nail polish bottle full of nuclear fallout, and a string of four white paper origami swans. The latter had been made by a little Japanese girl who was dying of radiation sickness and who had lain in a bed near Dorothea in the makeshift tent hospital where the singer had found herself stranded after the horrific Hiroshima bombing. All were relics of the Diva's fatal visit to that doomed Japanese city and testaments to the truth that such bombs must never dropped again!

"You will carry on your mother's vision and battle, Hellene, my little dove. God wills you too," Max Schwan murmured softly though with solid conviction during one of his mourn-

154

ing ceremonies which was ultimately an affirmation of life, life without the threat of nuclear war!

True to this peace vision, his daughter would grow stronger and in the decades to come would work to promote everything her dear mother had stood for.

FINIS

REDEEMED

Rocket Scientist Dr. Gustav Gessler knew what he didn't like and what he didn't like was the regime Adolph Hitler had created. But the blue-eyed, goateed little man hadn't always felt that way. He had been one of those who had originally voted Der Führer in as Chancellor. Dr. Gessler had then applauded the Nazi Government's social reforms, like the work programs, the building of the massive Autobahn highways, and the vast boost given to industry and science. Indeed, he had gotten his engineering position at the Dusseldorf Missile Plant through a government financed program.

Then Hitler had spoiled it all by poisoning his achievements with anti- Semitism. This turned Dr. Gessler's stomach. Before the Nazi's had began their volley of racial and religious persecutions, he had a lot of close Jewish friends. One whom he was particularly fond of was Johan Gilderberg. The two of them had been friends since grade school. They had gone on to attend the same Bavarian university and the same classes in aeronautics and engineering. From there, both of them and their families had made plans for them to go to work together at the Dusseldorf Missile Plant.

Then came the awful day, less than a week before Gustav Gessler and Johan Gilderberg were to graduate, that the brown uniformed Gestapo came knocking on the door of the dormitory room they shared.

"Don't worry, dear friend, the angel will come down from

the sky and rescue you," said Gessler as his equally short, though darker companion was led roughly away. Gilderberg smiled. There was a special secret between them that only they knew about.

The Nazi stormtroopers scoffed.

"There are no angels, silly fool," one of them said mockingly.

But you are wrong, you brute. Were the unspoken thoughts behind Dr. Gessler's bespectacled eyes.

Since that day, Gessler had continued in his studies and then gone on to construct the device he and his friend had drawn up the blue print for when both of them were still teenagers in trade school. But it was lonely work, even though the pudgy, though handsome scientist had plenty of assistants and fellow scientists to help him in the actual building of his and Gilderberg's invention. Then there were the ubiquitous Gestapo men with their trim suits and hateful swastika lapel pins. How Gessler loathed them and did his best to keep out of their way.

Gessler was lonely in the teaming Nazi bee hive of the missile plant because he felt surrounded by potential enemies, and more significantly, because he missed his dear friend. To ease his loneliness, he contrived to keep secretly in touch with Gilderberg, who was by then languishing in the brutal conditions of the Mitteldorf labor camp. He did this by a special private courier who acted at terrible risk to them both and herself as the go-between taking messages to the dark-haired little fellow. These reports were usually verbal ones.

This clandestine messenger was one of Dr. Gessler's technical assistants at the missile plant. She happened to be a pretty, petite lady named Gundran Fedder, who always wore her blonde hair in braids coiled on either side of her head. She was the only one of his team whom he had taken into his confidence about his Jewish friend. She was also the lady whom he was to eventually marry, so her labor as Gessler's courier was one of love. What's more, she had known Gilderberg since childhood as well and, like her short, blond fiancé, counted him as a friend worth taking any risk for.

The message Fraulein Fedder had been bringing to Gilderberg was the same. "Have courage. The Angel is coming together," she would assure him. Indeed, it was.

Then came the bright day when Fraulein Fedder brought her Hebrew friend the message he had been praying would come.

"The angel is ready!"

When Fraulein Fedder told him this, Gilderberg had to restrain himself from shouting with joy and tossing his red and white prisoner's cap to the wooden ceiling of his cold, dingy barracks like place of confinement. Soon, he would have to fear neither exposure nor confinement any longer.

On the same day that Dr. Gessler's fiancée brought their imprisoned friend this good news, the blond rocket engineer was supervising the last aerial test of his invention in the missile factory's cavern-like underground wind tunnel. When this was done, he was called into the plant supervisor's office.

"It is time for you to launch your device in our air war

against Britain! Is it ready?" spoke the supervisor behind his neat wooden desk. Like most minor Nazi Party functionaries, he was a thin middle-aged man who wore a gray uniform and a monocle.

"Yes, Herr Braume, it is ready and it will be launched on schedule," replied Gessler who added slyly to himself, *But not in the way you think.*

Later that day, the scientist, accompanied by Fraulein Fedder, climbed aboard his manned rocket, The Silver Angel, which was more officially known as the V-4. They overpowered the young luftwaffe colonel who had already gotten its engine started and threw him out into the hangar. Then before anyone could stop them, they were off with a deafening roar.

Dr. Gessler and his pretty assistant were headed straight for their home village of Mittenwald in Bavaria. Predictably, the German warplanes soon scrambled into the sky and tried to stop their 300 foot silvery rocket, but neither their bullets nor their bombs could put so much as a dent in its haul which was made of a metal alloy of immense strength that Gessler himself had invented. Then too, the shells shot from the cannons he had equipped it with ensured no mere plane could remain in the sky against it.

Traveling at a speed greater than any airplane could, Gessler and his lady soon reached their forested village. There they picked up twelve of Gessler's cousins, all of whom were short, blond, and brilliant like himself. These twelve included six men and six women. From there, Gessler and Fraulein Fedder flew on to keep an important promise.

A few hours later, they were hovering over the brick, wood, and barbed wire that made up the ugly prison camp where Gilderberg was confined. Quickly, their craft's cannons eliminated the camp's armed guards and the Messerschmidt planes which were still coming in droves..

"The Angel is here! The Angel is here!" Gilderberg shouted with glee to his five surviving fellow Jewish prisoners. In his excitement, he hurled his round striped cap in the air.

Then a chain ladder fell down to them and they all climbed on board the rocket to safety. When Gessler saw his old friend, he left the controls to Fraulein Fedder and walked over to hug him.

"Gustav, you look great and I look terrible!" said Gilderberg as he returned Gessler's embrace.

Indeed, the brutalities of life in the Mitteldorf camp had changed his appearance drastically! His small frame was as thin as a rail because the guards had half-starved him while forcing him to do hard labor. His bespectacled brown eyes were sunken and had black circles around them due to mal-nutrition. His wealth of curly black hair had been shaved off completely as a safeguard against lice, which were a bother anyway.

"We'll feed you and fatten you up and pretty soon you'll be your handsome old self again," Gessler reassured his rescued companion as he choked back his tears. Fraulein Fedder turned around from the controls and smiled at them both.

Gilderberg and the other six Jews were then given clean clothes and shown to their quarters in the rocket where they showered and then relaxed before a delicious koshered meal. It being Saturday, all of them prepared for evening worship services which Gessler, though a staunch Roman Catholic, was happy to supply the wine and candles for.

As all of this took place, The Silver Angel flew on to its next destination – the Rabengrau women's labor camp where Gilderberg's own fiancée, Annaliese Krane, was interned. Once there, the still lovely if bedraggled raven haired flower of Hebrew womanhood was rescued, along with six others equally charming. The Jewish prayer service aboard The Silver Angel that evening would be full and joyous.

As the fourteen Jews worshiped, their two Christian benefactors sped their rocket into a higher and higher trajectory, its gleaming nose pointing sharply upward. It continued to swiftly climb up past the clouds, up through and beyond each layer of the Earth's atmosphere. Then the starry void embraced it as it left the planet's orbit. Still it continued its upward climb.

"We are going to fulfill our boyhood dream, Johan. We are going to build a homeland where Christians and Jews can all celebrate their own and each other's cultures. Where our peoples will settle their differences through reasoning and talking together rather than through war," said Gessler to Gilderberg the next morning as both of them breakfasted on poppy seed muffins and mocha coffee.

"Yes, my friend, you are rescuing us all with the rocket you built. You are Noah and this is the Ark," said Gilderberg without a trace of irony. His fairer friend blushed.

"Thank you," he told the little dark fellow with touching

modesty, "though I hardly think I'm equal to that great man of God. But by the same token, perhaps if I'm Noah, then you are the promised Hebrew Messiah."

It was then Gilderberg's turn to blush. Then he laughed, "No, I don't think so. But I'm going to see that my people and yours have a truly new start on Mars."

"To Mars then."

"Yes, onward to Mars."

At that they clicked their brown coffee mugs together. Their Angel kept on with its upward climb. They knew that their journey through space would be a long one – up to three years. Wisely, Gessler had made sure that his massive craft was well stocked with every sort of necessary provision.

Onward and upward The Silver Angel sped. Days became weeks, weeks became months, and before any of them knew it, a whole year had passed. Meanwhile, its forty-two passengers carried on with their lives, working, playing, resting, and worshiping and doing so admirably well considering how confined their quarters happened to be. People were bonding closer together despite racial, cultural, and religious differences. Since the ratio of men to women was what it was, it wasn't surprising that several couples paired off and then married.

It was good then that there was a Catholic Priest and a Rabbi on board to perform these rites. Indeed, Gessler and Gilderberg had planned it that way. As it was, the Catholic Priest was Gessler's own cousin, Joachim. As the journey unfolded, the scientist clung to his faith so that he could maintain his inner strength and help his passengers stay strong in theirs

One morning Gessler kneeled, as he often did, before the shrine that he had erected to Christ and the Virgin Mary in his private quarters. The centerpiece of this small place of worship was a gold and ivory crucifix on the wall and a wooden pedestal beneath it which was draped with a scarlet silk cloth embroidered all over with gold thread crosses. In the center of this pedestal was a statue of the Virgin Mary made of the finest Dresden china. On the right side of this was a photo of the most recent Pope, Pius XII, in a gilted frame, while on the left side was a pot of flourishing red tea roses.

"Holy Mary mother of Jesus, please guide me to make a better life for myself and my friends," he prayed earnestly.

Than he slowly looked up and saw that the faces on the crucifix, the statue of The Virgin, and the black and white photo of the Pope seemed to all be smiling down on him as if to say, "Don't worry, my son, we are here for you."

Just then, Gessler felt a hand on his shoulder. He turned around to see his Jewish friend smiling at him in the same reassuring way. Truly, his prayer was being answered abundantly.

Finally, at long last, the silvery metal rocket touched down on the swirling red sands of Mars. As soon as the mighty engine had died down, Gessler and Gilderberg stepped out into a vast desert of rusty sand and pebbles. Beyond them were lofty red mountains and above them was a sky as ruddy as an eternal sunset. They pitched their flags. The one Gessler placed in the sand was red, black, and gold, and embellished with the German Eagle or Reichsadler. Gilder-berg's was blue with a silver Star of David.

These two leaders were, of course, wearing tin can-like environmental suits which Gessler had designed especially for surviving in the raw, untamed environment of Mars. After planting the flags, they and the others set out to tame it.

Using their rocket as a home base, the settlers from Earth used a small plane to seed Mars' orange clouds in order to create a breathable atmosphere for the entire planet. The skies above them, however, would always have a rusty, rather than blue look. The air would also remain somewhat thinner and colder than their planet of origin, but they would adapt. They used magnetic charges to make Mars' gravity less dense and more fit to live in. Then they tapped the red planet's vast wealth of underground water reservoirs to create lakes, rivers, and streams.

With the foundation of a newly inhabitable world established, the Mars settlers went on to move their gardens from their rocket to the surface of the planet itself. They had already been growing all manner of eatable plants in the controlled environment of the Silver Angel's huge terrarium and had been growing them quite well.

First, the colonists replanted their orchards and vegetables in Quonset hut green houses. Then when the Mars environment was judged to be more friendly, everything was shifted directly to the newly enriched soil of Mars itself. New seeds were planted too. Soon patches of the Martian terrain began to grow lush and verdant.

On the heels of agriculture came industry in the form of mines, foundaries, factories, and shops for Mars has vast natural resources. One of these is iron which is what makes it "The Red Planet". Since industry always requires some form of exchange to keep it going, the new Martian's leaders introduced a barter system early on.

The two colony heads, Gessler and Gilderberg, also had distinctive villages established for their peoples and each one was highly characteristic of the people who lived there. Not surprisingly, the German villages were distinctly German with buildings having ornately carved shutters and the people wearing lederhosen and dirndl skirts. The Jewish towns were not that different since Gilderberg's people were largely German-Jewish. Nevertheless, if one could have visited there they would have soon found that Yiddish and Hebrew were spoken in place of German and synagogues stood in place of the catholic churches.

Although cultural distinctiveness was encouraged, separatism and national egotism was not. Cultural sharing was the norm on all sides and would become more so as time went by. Therefore, although the German villages started out markedly gentile and the Jewish ones markedly Jewish, some of them began to diversify and incorporate the features of both religious cultures with the most charming results. In truth, it was charming to see Hasidic Jewish ladies in traditional long gowns and lacy scarves dining at a German cafe or a German Catholic priest drinking koshered beer with a cluster of rabbi in a Jewish community. Naturally, intermarriages happened often and were always rejoiced in when they did.

As a further part of the new civilization's spirit of peace and brotherly and sisterly goodwill, war, or any other form of violence for that matter, was strictly forbidden as a means of settling differences. Instead, disputes between people and groups of people were settled by a panel of Councilors who listened to both sides and then gave the fairest and most impartial advice possible under the circumstances. Their advice was final and their decisions were the law for the entire planet. Each panel of Councilors was comprised of two Jews and two Catholics and there was one in each town.

All of these developments of Martian Civilization took place over a period of many decades and, what's more, took place under the very noses and telescopes of Earth's major scientists. They are still going on strong today. But no one nor anything from Earth can detect the quaint villages and flourishing orchards which Gessler, Gilderberg, and their friends have established on Mars, because every time the "Martians" sense they are being spied on, they throw up a heavy cloud of red dust which nothing can penetrate. It is just was well.

FINIS

TWO BROTHERS

In the state of Utah, a boychild was born to Jessica and Joe Steckborn. They named him Job. This was November 11, 1955. At a very young age, this boy, who was sturdy and blond, showed a deep love for animals. From the time he could walk, Job collected numerous pets of all kinds of animals. While other kids played doctor, he liked to play pretend veterinarian. Smart and outgoing already, he made friends with people of all ages. His parents were devote Mormons and raised him to be too.

Then in 1957 his brother Todd was born and Job's happy boyhood began to turn bitter. Right from the start, this brother seemed intent on usurping all of their parent's love and attention and he quickly became their special favorite. Job was left out in the cold emotionally. But that wasn't the worst thing about Todd. This chubby, shifty-eyed youngster behaved badly toward everyone and was often bad tempered and disobedient. As soon as he learned how to talk, Todd lied like a rug. What's more he was vile towards animals. One evening, Job watched him load a bag full of kittens into a smoldering burn barrel. He tried to rescue them, but was only able to save one. This kitten would be blind in one eye for the rest of his life because of his burns. Job named him Levi and took him on as his pet. From then on, Job managed to protect the feline from his brother.

At school Job did exceptionally well with a special aptitude for Spelling, History, and English. He was liked by his teachers who saw great potential in him and found many friends among his classmates. He had serious intentions of studying to be a veterinarian for real. Todd, on the other hand, did poorly at his lessons and didn't seem to care. He was predictably disobedient to his teachers and got into a lot of fights with the other children. Still his parents favored him over Job.

Todd seemed to spend most of his time torturing and killing animals, especially dogs and cats. Cats, he torched by one method or another. The dogs he targeted were invariably Pomeranians since they resembled cats to him. Them he killed by knifing up in true Jack The Ripper fashion. When Job told their parents about his brother's atrocities with animals, he was cautioned to shut up and mind his own business. In their minds, Todd could do no wrong.

The two brothers entered teenhood and Todd went from beating up on the family pets to beating up his doting parents. Still, Jessica and Joe Steckborn remained blind to their youngest son's growing proclivity toward violence. While Job studied and helped with family chores, Todd joined a street gang and was often into fights, drinking, and stealing. He was already displaying all of the traits of a dangerous psychopath. Some said he had inherited these evil tendencies from his mother's murderous 16th Century ancestor, Christman Genippteinga who terrorized Germany during The Little Ice Age.

Then came the draft and Job joined the Army, while Todd burned his draft card and ran off to The Yucatan and formed a cult. As cult leader he went from making blood sacrifices of dogs and cats to sacrificing horses. Then it was very young virgin girls.

While in Vietnam Job was part of the "Black Horse" 11th Cavalry. He worked as a dog handler and then excelled as a tank driver and helicopter pilot. In his position as a tank driver, he later took part in an important rescue mission involving some US soldiers trapped by the enemy in a part of Cambodia called ironically, "The Dog's Head". After the war, he was transferred to Germany where he remained part of the 11th Cavalry and excelled as a "Sapper" or explosives handler. But despite of these heroic accomplishments, his parents only wrote once and never sent him care packages or phoned. On the other hand, they knew of Todd's whereabouts and remained in close touch with him, all the while keeping his location a secret from the authorities. They even sent him money.

After doing his time in the service, Job returned to America where married a lovely, golden-brown-tressed girl from Saginaw, Michigan named Alice Barry. Together, they had twins – a boy and a girl. They also took on a lot of pets of different kinds. Job finally studied to be a veterinarian and opened his own clinic in Flint, Michigan.

Then gruesome things started to happen. The family pets began to end up dead and horribly mutilated on Job's doorstep. Then his wife and children vanished. A note left behind explained that his brother, Todd, was behind it all. With some brilliant sleuthing, Job was able to find his brother's whereabouts and demanded to know where Alice and the twins were. His brother explained that they were all fine, but would remain hidden until Job met with him at a specified Mayan pyramid deep in the Yucatan jungle. Job agreed to meet him and got directions to the ancient edifice. When the brothers met, Job offered Todd a brotherly reconciliation, but Todd lunged at him with a Mayan obsidian dagger, a knife once used in that ancient people's blood sacrifices.

As he leaped and gashed, the berserk man shouted at Job that he needed to kill him to rid his mind of the voices that tormented him every moment of his life. But Job was quick and able to dodge him and fight back. Just as Job was about ready to knock Todd down with a swift punch, a one-eyed cat with sand-colored fur suddenly appeared out of nowhere. With a loud yowel, the cat leaped upon Todd's face and soon had him on the floor clawing his face and neck to bloody shreds. As Todd lay writhing, the cat jumped up again, knocking a lantern to the floor. Everything caught fire and explosions began. Job found his family and fled.

A month later, the newly widowed Jessica Steckborn was at the site of the devastated Mayan pyramid. Amongst the rubble, she discovered the charred body of her evil favorite son. Hugging this sooty skeleton to her bosom, she burst into tears and her wails filled the Mexican jungle. Then she happened to glance over at one of the former pyramid's remaining walls. On it she saw, or imagined she saw, the impression of a cat! Whichever was the case, Jessica received a jolt of fear in her heart so intense that she fell dead over the remains of the son that she had so foolishly doted on. And as she died, she died alone with only the jungle birds and animals as witnesses.

FINIS

BETTE

Bette Strassemaus was a threadbare poor young female editor of a small newspaper living with her Schnauzer dog, Pryfer, in the slum section of West Berlin in the early 1980s. In spite of her talents, Bette was living below poverty level and was single because she was homely and somewhat addled mentally and emotionally.

One day, Bette was hired by a powerful witch from Mittenwald named Lurlina to write a poem in her honor. In payment, Lurlina gave Bette a magic ring.

When she put on this ring and rubbed its ruby setting, a small dragon appeared and offered to grant her every wish. Bette wished for beauty and a stable mind and emotions. She also wished for her newspaper to be a big success all over West Germany. The little dragon swished his tail and all three wishes were instantly granted.

Having become a success in life at last, Bette began courting James Steffisburg, the handsome, brilliant, American Military Envoy to West Germany's Chancellor, Alaric Schwan. Unfortunately, the evil statuesque Lurlina had designs on him herself, though more for reasons of political ambition than love. She also had her eyes on attaining the office of Vice Chancellor. With the aid of their feminine charms and their dragons, the two women began competing for Steffisburg's hand in marriage. Bette ultimately foiled Lurlina by taking control of her larger more powerful dragon.

She did this by finding his cave and then stealing the jewel from his forehead. Bette then had this black diamond made into a necklace that she would wear always. Shortly after securing this powerful amulet, Bette married Steffisburg and for their wedding present the big dragon built them a wonderful palatial mansion, a far more magnificent one than that of the Chancellor himself.

Though prevented from winning Steffisburg, Lurlina was able to fulfill her other ambition – that of gaining the position of Vice Chancellor. She then set out to usurp more and more control over Chancellor Schwan. In her new position of great power, she tried to seduce Steffisburg, but he rebuffed her and remained true to Bette. Finally, Lurlina managed to steal Bette's necklace and thereby regain control of her own dragon.

Lurlina ordered this dragon to take Bette and James Steffisburg's mansion, along with all of its contents, to a secluded piece of acreage that she owned in the wooded area near Mittenwald. Luckily, Bette still had the magic ring and was able to summon her smaller dragon. Although the dragon of the ring could not directly undo any of the magic of the bigger dragon, he was able to transport Bette and her husband to Mittenwald where they recovered the necklace and killed Lurlina in battle. Now that Bette had both dragons on magical harnesses again, she had them return her mansion to its proper place.

However, there was more trouble on the horizon for the former lady journalist and her man. The witch's more powerful and evil brother, Winsoln Auslaugen, happened to be a powerful terrorist leader hiding out in East Germany. To avenge his sister's death and put his own power seeking agenda into action, Auslaugen began sending squads of red terrorist assassins and saboteurs after the man and wife with the object of killing them. But with the help of Bette's dragons, this terrorist wave was discovered and foiled. Auslaugen's other plot to replace Schwan, through political chicanery, with a young German-Turkish fellow was also brought to light. For reasons of political expediency, the Soviet and East German top officials put pressure on Auslaugen to stop his terrorist activities and give up his designs on interfering in West Germany's internal affairs.

   With peace having returned to West Germany, The Steffisburg's and Schwan had a summit conference in West Berlin with the then US President, Hank Robins, and everyone but their foes east of the Berlin Wall lived happily ever after.

FINIS

SUMMER GREEN

It was early summer and Chancellor Alaric Schwan's country estate was covered with greenery. Everywhere, the oak, maple, and linden trees bore thick emerald leaves and the grass underfoot was a soft jade carpet.

On this special, minty green morning, Schwan was with his wife, April, out on a horseback jaunt into the leafy bowers and verdant shaded pathways which the forested countryside of West Germany had now become.

Small, blond, handsome Schwan kept a stable of fifty thoroughbred horses for just such excursions. These included many unusual and outstanding breeds from Arabians to Lipizzaners, so he and his lady had quite a variety to choose from. But the lovely little redhead had been so eager to ride that she only took a moment to decide.

"I'll take this one," said April as she pointed a dainty fair finger at a cream colored Arabian mare.

"Fine, my love, then I will ride the sorrel stallion," decided Herr Schwan.

Fritz Jagger, the natty, brown-haired Stable Groom, helped the Chancellor and his wife as they saddled up. Then they were on their way! For hours, they rode through hill and dale, across pine spread mountains and through cool forests, each vista becoming more lush than the next.

Eventually, they came to the heart of the Grunewald Forest where the pine and spruce were so thick that the whole region seemed to be sunk in a deep green twilight. In the middle of this bosky shade stood the log cabin of a man whom Herr Schwan knew well. The recluse's name was Walter Boehm and he was a metalwork artist. With extraordinary skill and fineness of detail, he made sculptures and figurines out of various types of metal. He also made plaques out of fine steel wire.

Alaric Schwan led April to Boehm's cabin where they hitched their horses to two nearby pines. Then the two travelers were greeted at the door by the slim, long-haired artist himself. He welcomed them both in and fed them strawberries and blueberries from his own berry patches, while showing them several examples of his fine art.

After Boehm was through with his impromptu art show, he asked Frau Schwan if he could make a plaque in her charming likeness.

"Yes, you may," she consented, somewhat flattered.

For the next half hour, April sat primly in one of Boehm's smoothly varnished spruce wood chairs as the metalworker deftly duplicated her curves and curls in the delicate steel wire with the aid of pliers, metal cutters, and soldering gun.

While he watched Boehm weave this fine plaque from a web of wire, Herr Schwan contemplated on how well it captured his woman's tender, but ardent beauty.

But not her fierce spirit, thought the Chancellor to himself with a bemused smile, one might as well try to tame a tempest in her native Michigan's Lake Superior.

FINIS

175

THE MAN ON A WHITE HORSE

It was an early summer morning and West German Chancellor Alaric Schwan awoke to the sweet scent of edelweiss wafting in through the window of his white marble schloss. With the vigor that can only come from good health, he climbed out of his four poster oaken bed with its white silk pillows, coverlets, and swan shaped throw pillows. As he stretched his arms and yawned in his fine, baritone voice, he admired the nearby Alpine Mountains which were still bathed in the crimson of dawn.

Suddenly, he smelled the coffee that his wife, April, had made in the kitchen downstairs. Ah, lovely April, always first with the coffee and the kisses, Schwan mused half-drowsily to himself with a fond smile. He would be joining her for both in a short while.

While still in his white silk pajamas, Schwan did a series of wake-up exercises. These included doing a set of push ups and some arm curls. He felt especially vigorous and full of well-being that morning because he had slept well and dreamed well. During the night, he had dreamed that every flower in Germany had become stamped with a prayer to The Virgin Mary. This miracle, according to his dream, had been brought about by the power of the The Holy Spirit so that every living soul in both Germanies would know the power of God and repent their sins, while spreading this benediction to the rest of all Europe.

When he was done with his morning work out, Schwan sat down on the edge of his bed, put on his aviator style photo gray glasses, and did a prayer ritual with his rosary. Then thoroughly cooled down and spiritually as well as physically refreshed, he went down the white carpeted stairs to his steam bath.

Following his steam bath, Schwan returned to his white velvet draped bedroom chamber and stood in front of a long, gold-framed mirror. As he briskly wiped away the tiny drops of moisture which clung like jewels to his fair flesh and pale blond hair, he briefly thanked God for having blessed him with strength and good health.

Suddenly, the mirror view of his own image was blotted out by a strange clouding. This was followed by the appearance of a man in shining armor. In his right hand was a flaming sword and on his back was a pair of white wings. For a moment, Chancellor Schwan was startled by the abruptness of the vision. Then he relaxed as he remembered who it was and why it had come.

"So Michael!" he said to the man in the mirror. "The time has come!"

"Yes, Alaric, the time has come!" agreed the apparition in a booming voice. Then it vanished!

Schwan knew then what he had to do. He finished drying himself off. Then he dressed and sat down to a breakfast of scrambled eggs, rye rolls with jam, and coffee with April. He enjoyed this hardy morning meal and the company of his lovely wife who treated him to a poem about edelweiss flowers. After eating his fill, he kissed her farewell and left the table while promising to call her while at work. But before going to his office at the Chancellery and starting the business of steering the ship of state that day, Schwan went to his schloss' armory. While there, he girded his waist with the Armor of Truth, his chest with the Breastplate of Righteousness, his feet with the Boots of The Gospel, and his head with the Helmet of Salvation – all in white tinted steel. For weapons, he took the Sword of The Spirit and the Shield of Faith.

Now in full battle array, Schwan selected a white war horse from his stables. He said a special prayer and his steed leaped up to the Heavens with a mighty neigh.

Higher and higher they climbed, past roofs, past birds, and past clouds. Finally, they came to a sunset ruddy, cloud carpeted zone where they encountered a sinister figure who was dressed in iron armor which was rusty red and who rode a roan horse. Schwan knew this to be Mephisto, the embodiment of all evil in Germany.

This demon charged at Schwan flinging at him the Darts of Deception. But Schwan was ready. He deflected each flaming missile with his sword and shield. At last, Mephisto ran out of darts and brought out his Sword of Satan.

A fast and furious series of parries and thrusts then began between the two beings as metal met metal with sparks like lightening and rumbles like thunder. At last, Schwan drove his blade, first into the bosom of the demon and then into the neck of his devil horse. The two of them gave a soul-tingling wail and then vanished.

God and good had won the battle.

FINIS

178

VETERAN'S DAY EVE

During a lull in the fighting at The Battle of The Bulge, a young American sergeant named Charles Shepherd found a German officer caught and struggling in a barbed wire fence. Feeling compassion for his foe, Sgt. Shepherd freed the man. The German, whose name was Colonel Franz Richter, thanked the American by pinning his own Iron Cross medal on his chest. Then he saluted him and walked on into the mist.

Forty years later, Charles Shepherd was an old man retired from both the service and a career as a tool and die man at the Burbank branch of California's Lockheed Corporation airplane plant. On the night of November 10, 1984, he had a mysterious dream. In it, he met Franz Richter again who was by this time in his declining years as well. The German died in Shepherd's arms as both of them reaffirmed their feelings of peace and goodwill. The next day, Shepherd inquired and learned that Herr Richter had actually died on the night of his dream.

A few days later, he attended the funeral of the man whom he had rescued so long ago and placed a wreath of edelweiss blossoms and linden branches on his grave.

FINIS

For a list of all available books by
Everlasting Publishing, please visit our website:
everlastingpublishing.org

www.ingramcontent.com/pod-product-compliance
Lightning Source LLC
Chambersburg PA
CBHW070025260626
47159CB00005B/1953